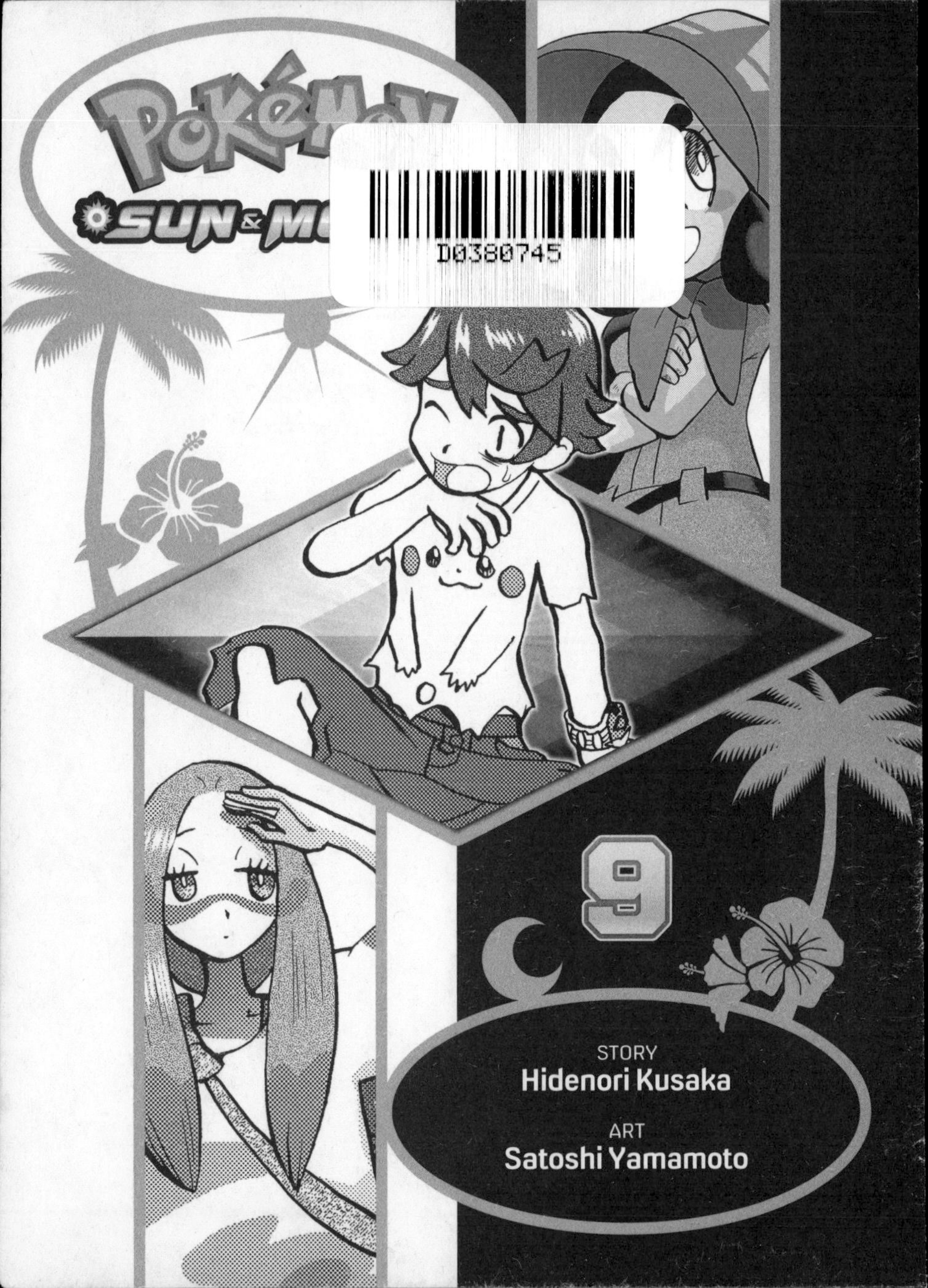
9
STORY
Hidenori Kusaka
ART
Satoshi Yamamoto

Introduction

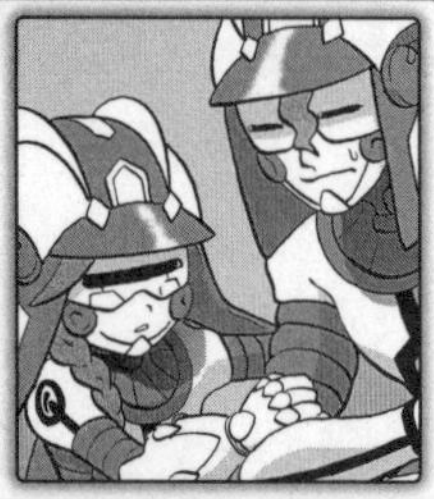

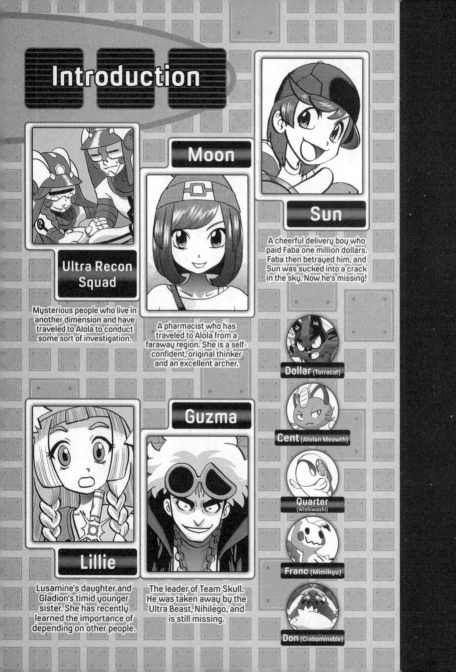

Ultra Recon Squad

Mysterious people who live in another dimension and have traveled to Alola to conduct some sort of investigation.

Moon

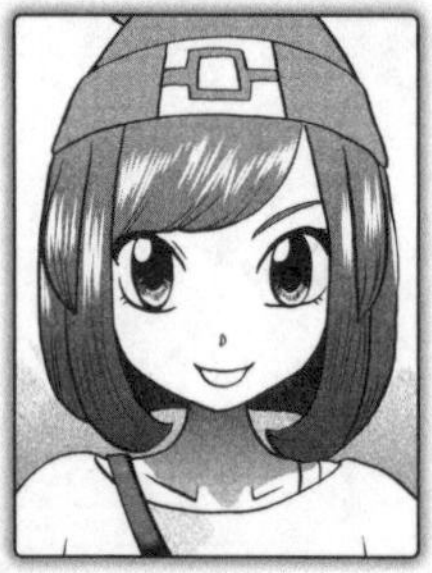

A pharmacist who has traveled to Alola from a faraway region. She is a self-confident, original thinker and an excellent archer.

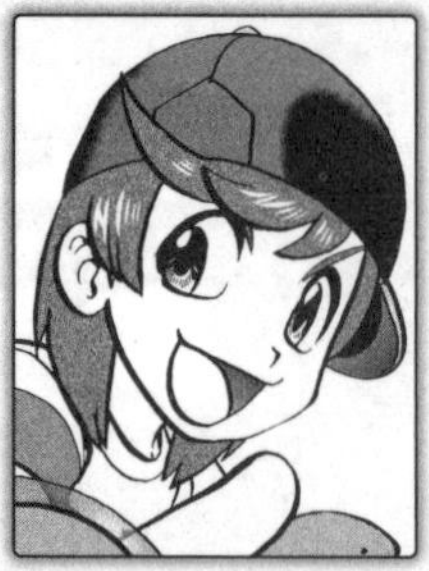

Sun

A cheerful delivery boy who paid Faba one million dollars. Faba then betrayed him, and Sun was sucked into a crack in the sky. Now he's missing!

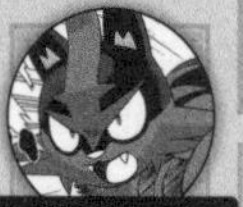

Dollar (Torracat)

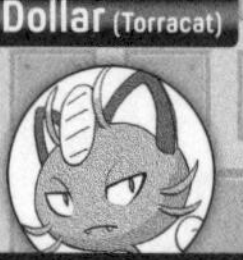

Cent (Alolan Meowth)

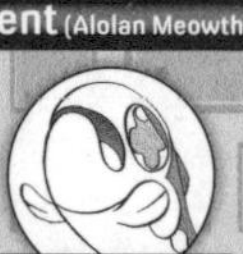

Quarter (Wishiwashi)

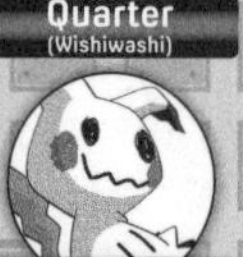

Franc (Mimikyu)

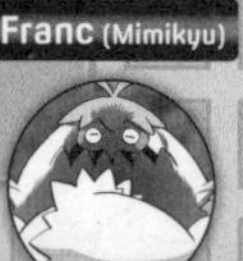

Don (Crabominable)

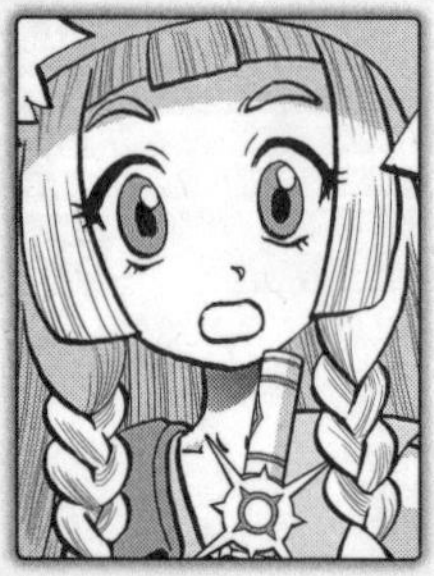

Lillie

Lusamine's daughter and Gladion's timid younger sister. She has recently learned the importance of depending on other people.

Guzma

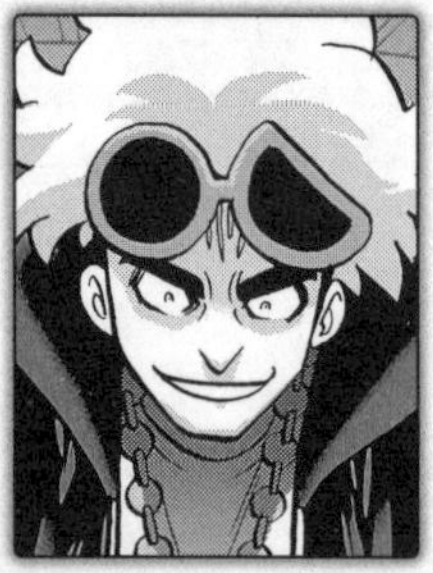

The leader of Team Skull. He was taken away by the Ultra Beast, Nihilego, and is still missing.

Character

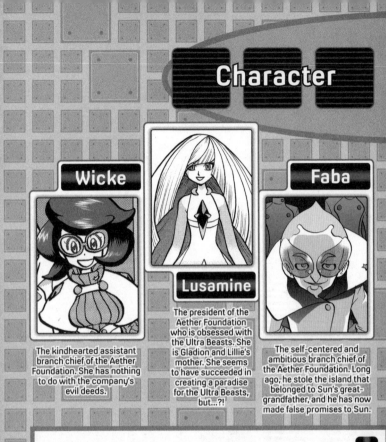

Wicke

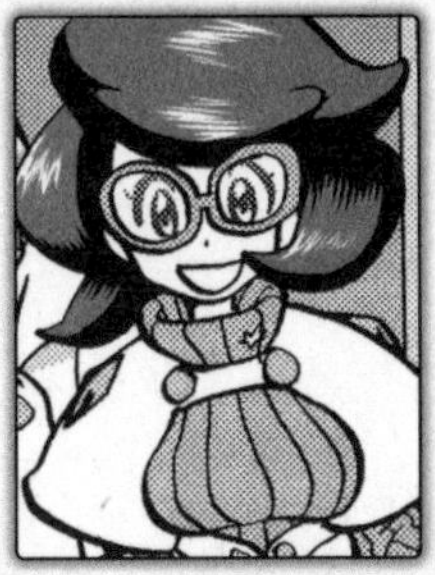

The kindhearted assistant branch chief of the Aether Foundation. She has nothing to do with the company's evil deeds.

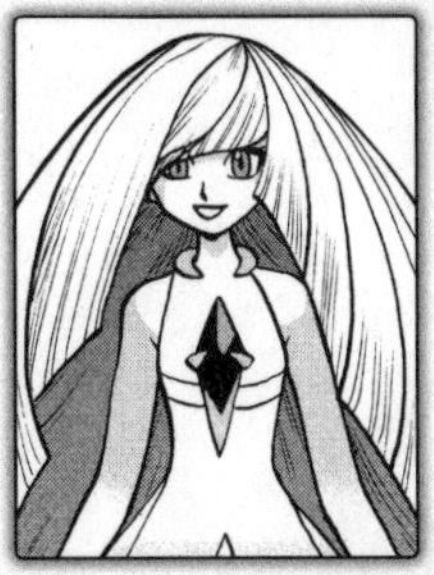

Lusamine

The president of the Aether Foundation who is obsessed with the Ultra Beasts. She is Gladion and Lillie's mother. She seems to have succeeded in creating a paradise for the Ultra Beasts, but...?!

Faba

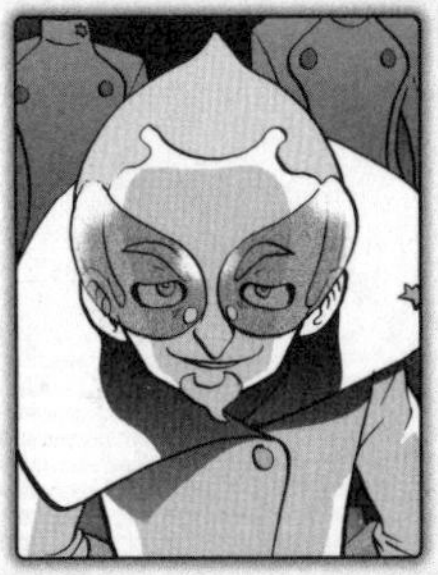

The self-centered and ambitious branch chief of the Aether Foundation. Long ago, he stole the island that belonged to Sun's great-grandfather, and he has now made false promises to Sun.

The Story Thus Far...

Moon, a pharmacist from another region, comes to the flower-filled vacation paradise of the Alola region, which consists of numerous tropical islands. While on an important errand, Moon meets Sun, who works various odd jobs and runs a delivery service to reach his goal of saving up a million dollars. When the Island Guardians of the Alolan Islands, called Tapu, become agitated, Sun is chosen to complete the island challenge to soothe the Tapus' anger. Moon comes along to help. Sun completes his island challenge by delivering a special Berry to the Tapu on different islands. While on the island of Poni, Sun and Moon play the legendary Sun and Moon flutes, causing two Cosmoem to transform into Solgaleo, the emissary of the sun, and Lunala, the emissary of the moon! Then a black claw reaches out from a crack in the sky, dragging Sun into it! Moon quickly chases after him, but where have they gone?!

CONTENTS

Zzt zzt... ♪

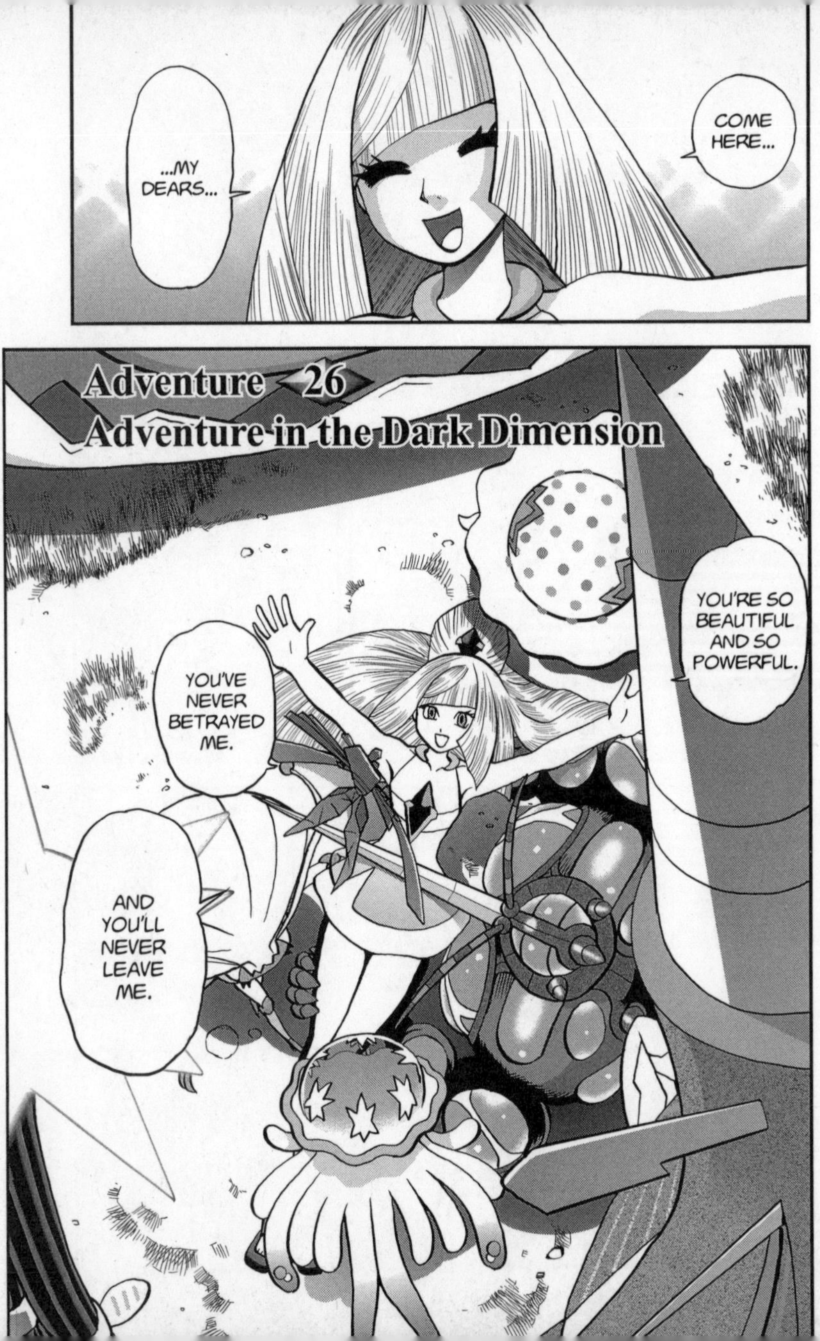
COME HERE...
...MY DEARS...
Adventure 26
Adventure in the Dark Dimension
YOU'RE SO BEAUTIFUL AND SO POWERFUL.
YOU'VE NEVER BETRAYED ME.
AND YOU'LL NEVER LEAVE ME.

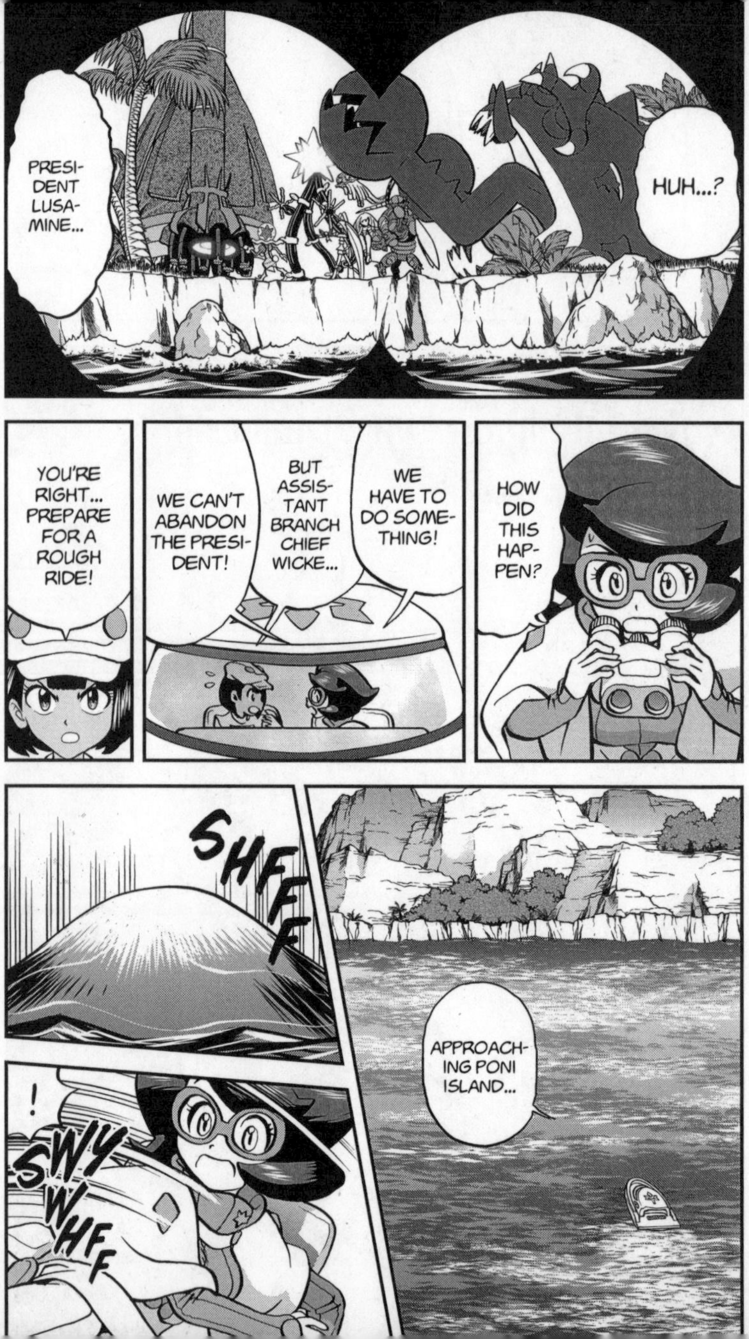
HUH...?
PRESIDENT LUSAMINE...
HOW DID THIS HAPPEN?
WE HAVE TO DO SOMETHING!
BUT ASSISTANT BRANCH CHIEF WICKE...
WE CAN'T ABANDON THE PRESIDENT!
YOU'RE RIGHT... PREPARE FOR A ROUGH RIDE!
APPROACHING PONI ISLAND...
SHFFF
!
SWY
SWHFF

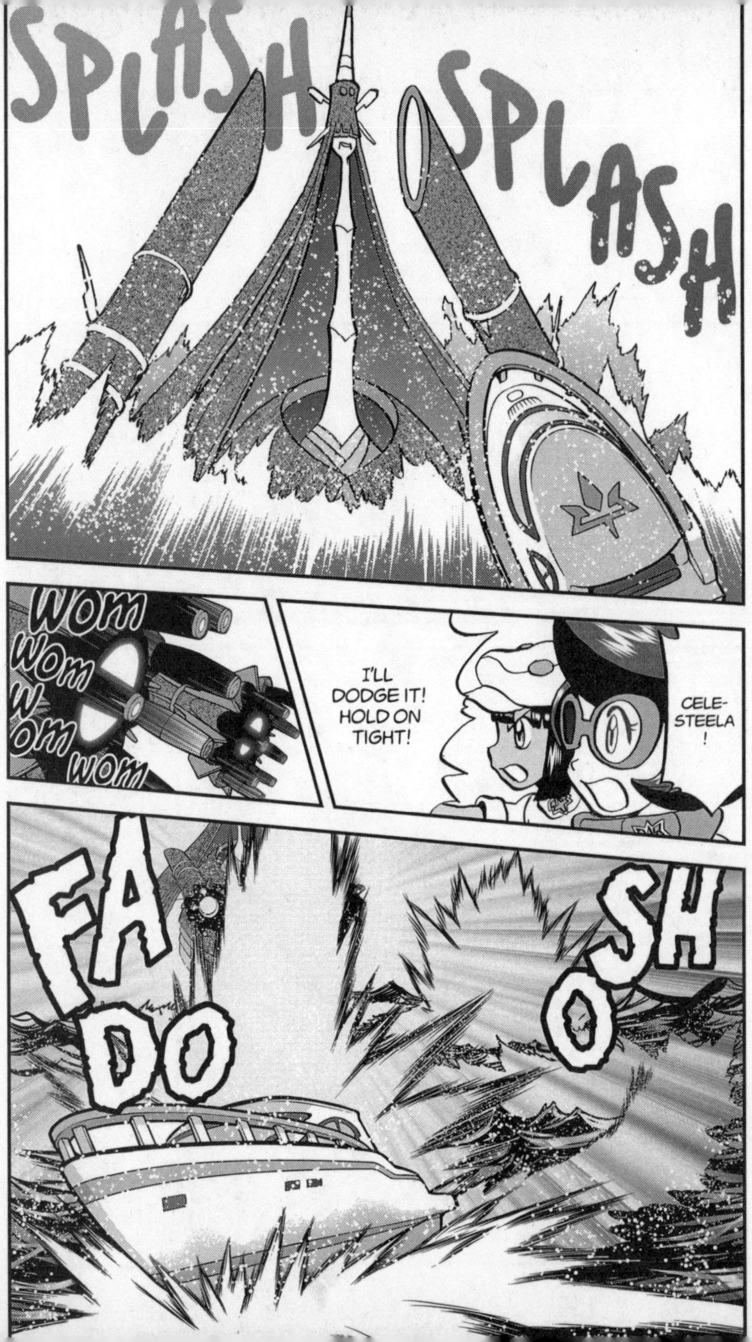
SPLASH
SPLASH
CELE-STEELA!
I'LL DODGE IT! HOLD ON TIGHT!
WOM WOM WOM WOM WOM
FADOOSH

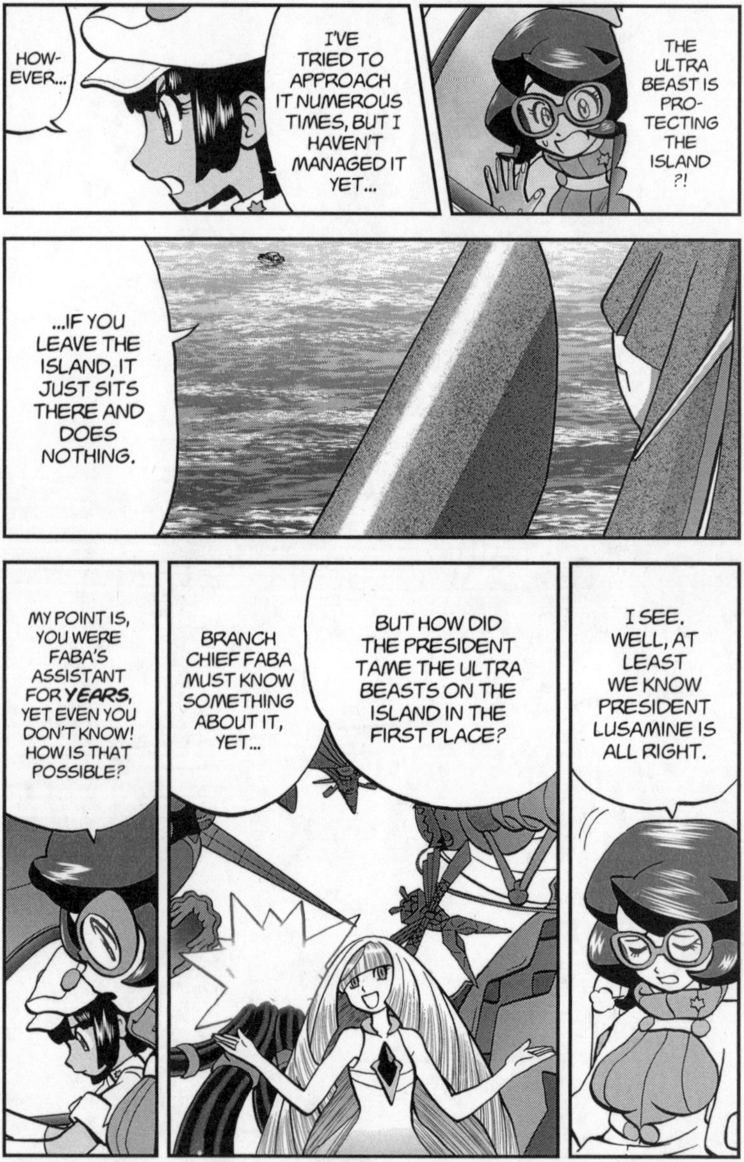
THE ULTRA BEAST IS PRO-TECTING THE ISLAND?!
I'VE TRIED TO APPROACH IT NUMEROUS TIMES, BUT I HAVEN'T MANAGED IT YET...
HOW-EVER...
...IF YOU LEAVE THE ISLAND, IT JUST SITS THERE AND DOES NOTHING.
I SEE. WELL, AT LEAST WE KNOW PRESIDENT LUSAMINE IS ALL RIGHT.
BUT HOW DID THE PRESIDENT TAME THE ULTRA BEASTS ON THE ISLAND IN THE FIRST PLACE?
BRANCH CHIEF FABA MUST KNOW SOMETHING ABOUT IT, YET...
MY POINT IS, YOU WERE FABA'S ASSISTANT FOR ***YEARS***, YET EVEN YOU DON'T KNOW! HOW IS THAT POSSIBLE?

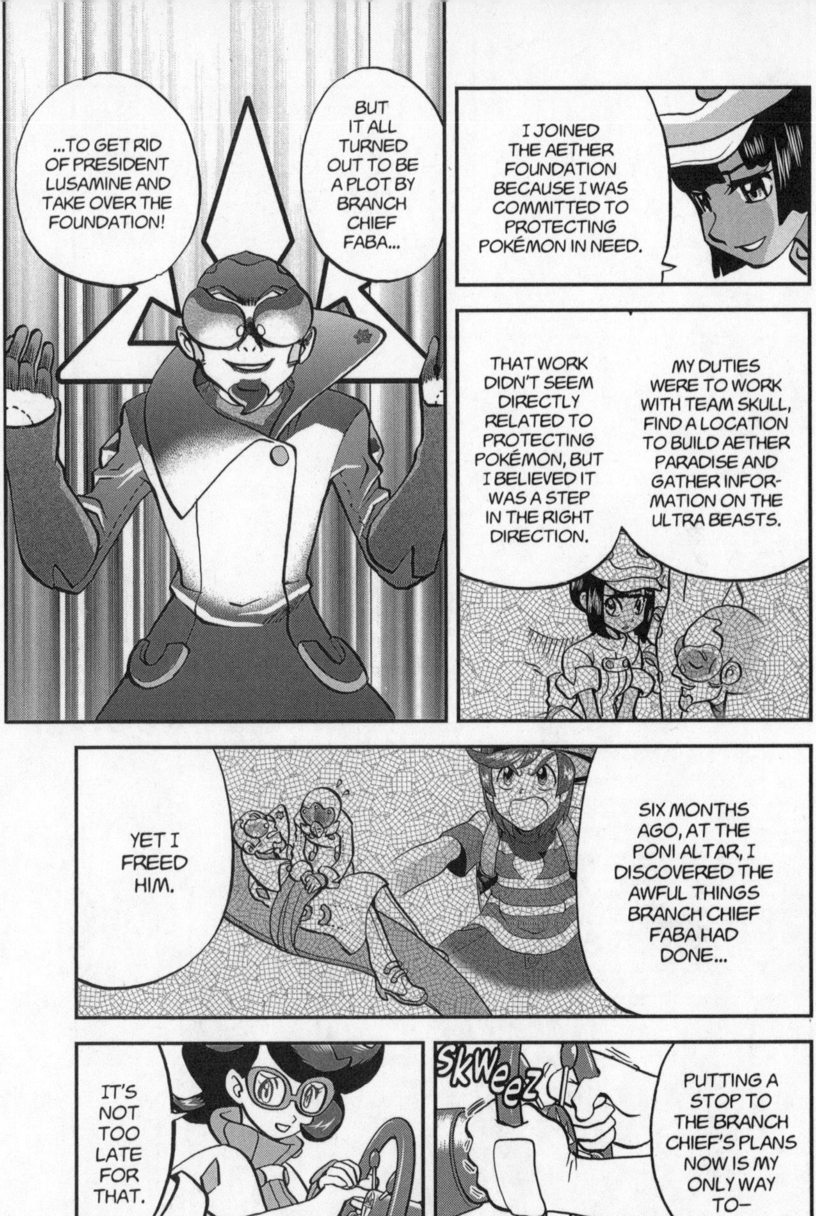
I JOINED THE AETHER FOUNDATION BECAUSE I WAS COMMITTED TO PROTECTING POKÉMON IN NEED.
MY DUTIES WERE TO WORK WITH TEAM SKULL, FIND A LOCATION TO BUILD AETHER PARADISE AND GATHER INFOR-MATION ON THE ULTRA BEASTS.
THAT WORK DIDN'T SEEM DIRECTLY RELATED TO PROTECTING POKÉMON, BUT I BELIEVED IT WAS A STEP IN THE RIGHT DIRECTION.
BUT IT ALL TURNED OUT TO BE A PLOT BY BRANCH CHIEF FABA...
...TO GET RID OF PRESIDENT LUSAMINE AND TAKE OVER THE FOUNDATION!
SIX MONTHS AGO, AT THE PONI ALTAR, I DISCOVERED THE AWFUL THINGS BRANCH CHIEF FABA HAD DONE...
YET I FREED HIM.
PUTTING A STOP TO THE BRANCH CHIEF'S PLANS NOW IS MY ONLY WAY TO—
SKWEEZ
IT'S NOT TOO LATE FOR THAT.

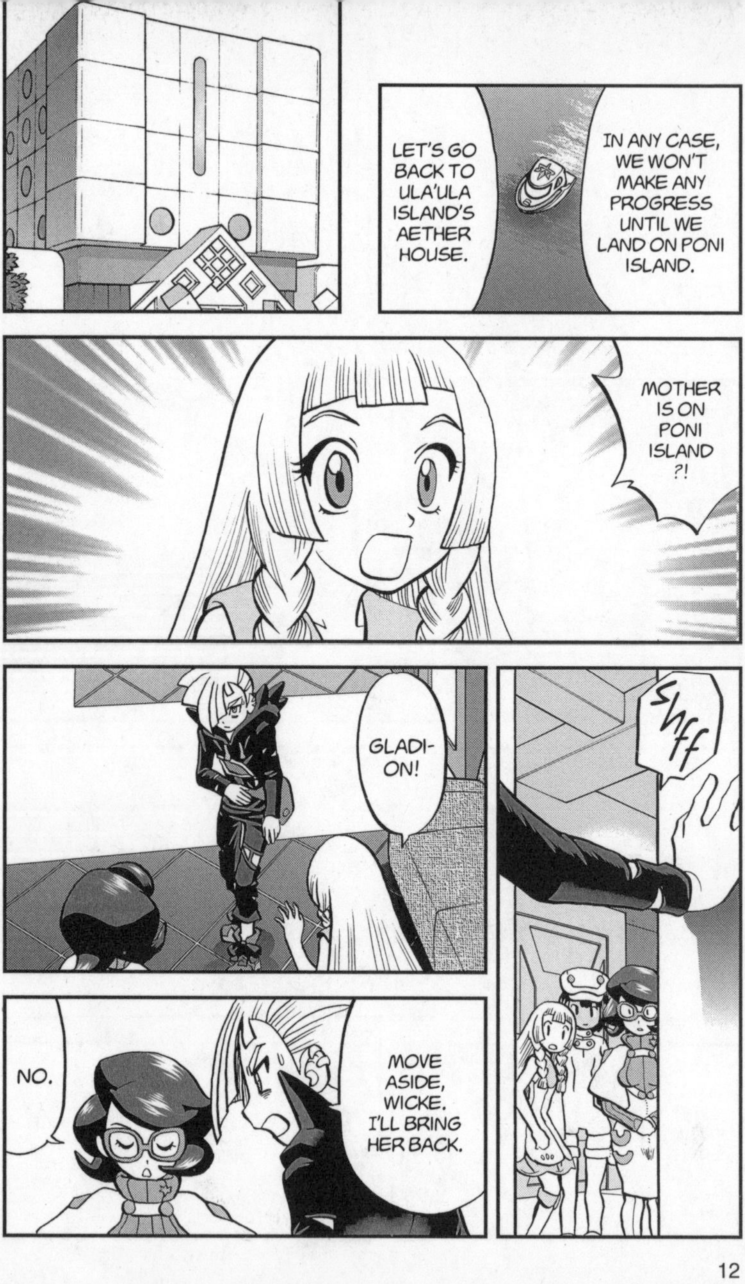
IN ANY CASE, WE WON'T MAKE ANY PROGRESS UNTIL WE LAND ON PONI ISLAND.
LET'S GO BACK TO ULA'ULA ISLAND'S AETHER HOUSE.
MOTHER IS ON PONI ISLAND ?!
SHFF
GLADI- ON!
MOVE ASIDE, WICKE. I'LL BRING HER BACK.
NO.

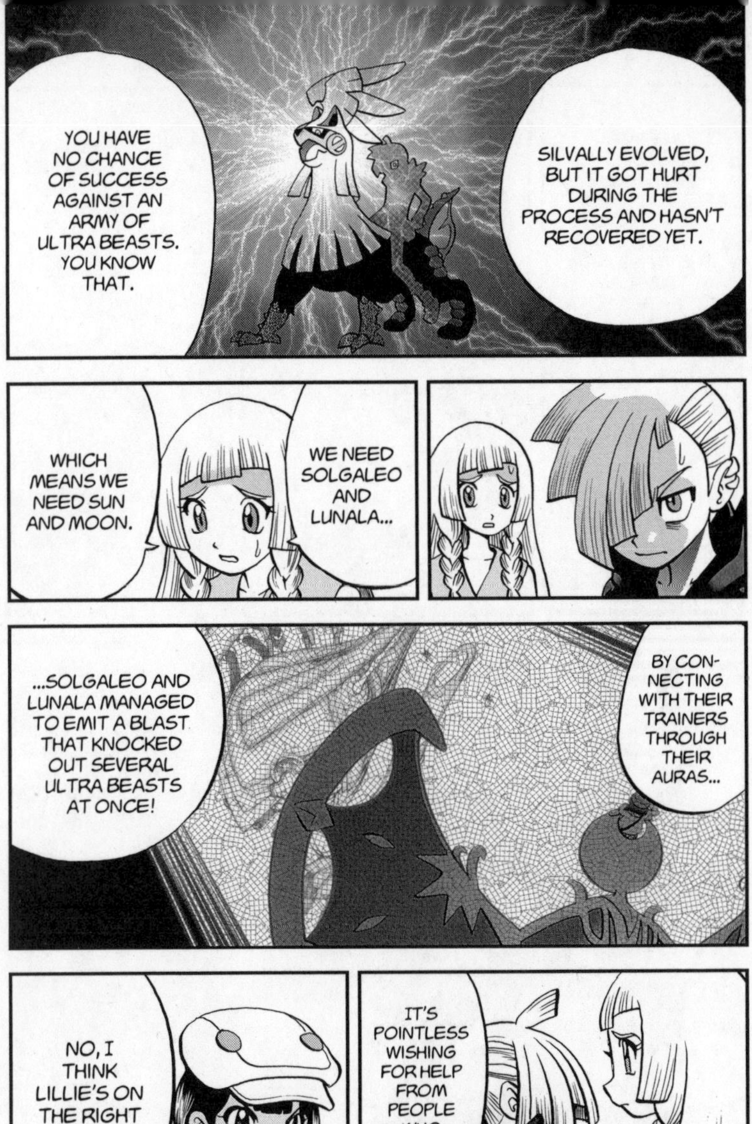

SILVALLY EVOLVED, BUT IT GOT HURT DURING THE PROCESS AND HASN'T RECOVERED YET.
YOU HAVE NO CHANCE OF SUCCESS AGAINST AN ARMY OF ULTRA BEASTS. YOU KNOW THAT.
WE NEED SOLGALEO AND LUNALA...
WHICH MEANS WE NEED SUN AND MOON.
BY CON-NECTING WITH THEIR TRAINERS THROUGH THEIR AURAS...
...SOLGALEO AND LUNALA MANAGED TO EMIT A BLAST THAT KNOCKED OUT SEVERAL ULTRA BEASTS AT ONCE!
IT'S POINTLESS WISHING FOR HELP FROM PEOPLE WHO AREN'T HERE...
NO, I THINK LILLIE'S ON THE RIGHT TRACK!

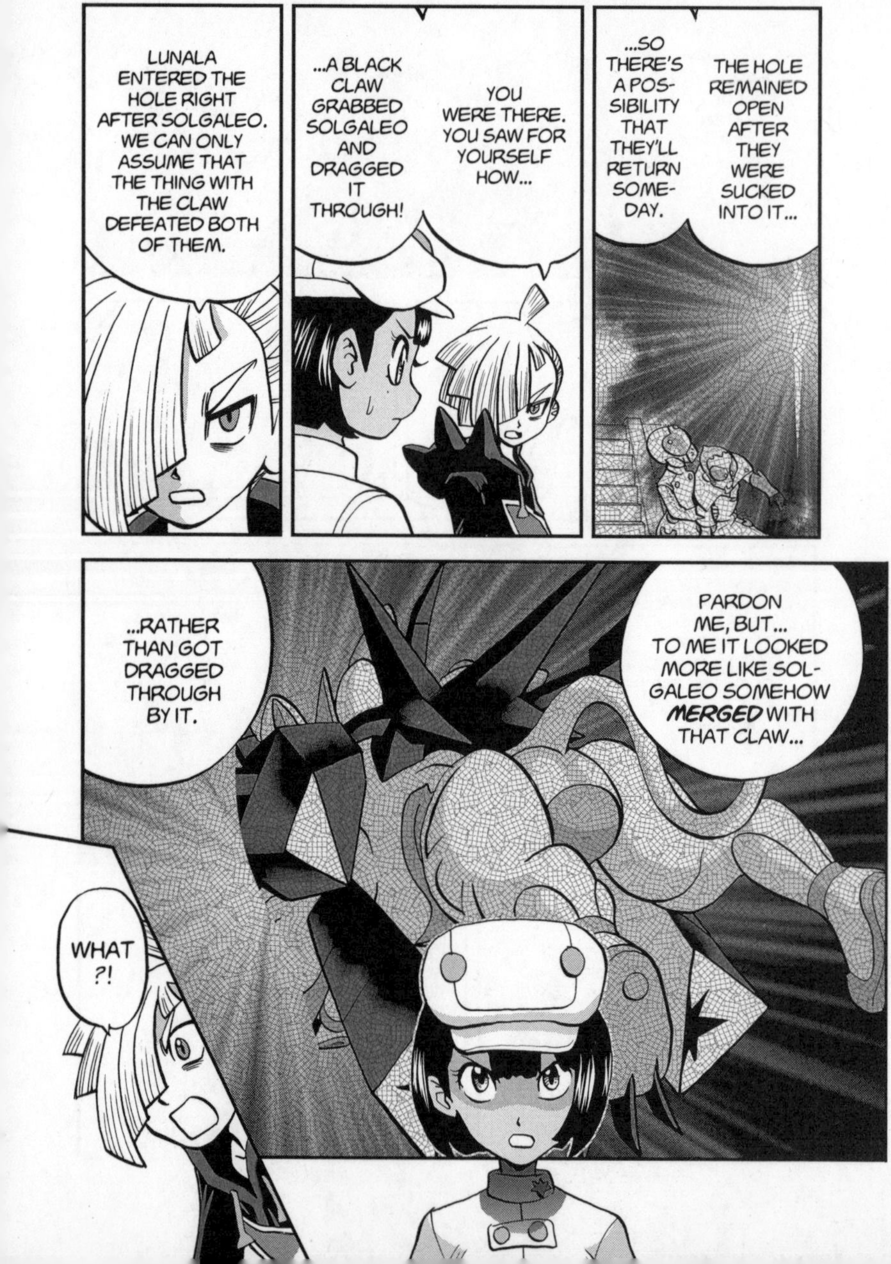
THE HOLE REMAINED OPEN AFTER THEY WERE SUCKED INTO IT...
...SO THERE'S A POS-SIBILITY THAT THEY'LL RETURN SOME-DAY.
YOU WERE THERE. YOU SAW FOR YOURSELF HOW...
...A BLACK CLAW GRABBED SOLGALEO AND DRAGGED IT THROUGH!
LUNALA ENTERED THE HOLE RIGHT AFTER SOLGALEO. WE CAN ONLY ASSUME THAT THE THING WITH THE CLAW DEFEATED BOTH OF THEM.
PARDON ME, BUT... TO ME IT LOOKED MORE LIKE SOL-GALEO SOMEHOW MERGED WITH THAT CLAW...
...RATHER THAN GOT DRAGGED THROUGH BY IT.
WHAT?!

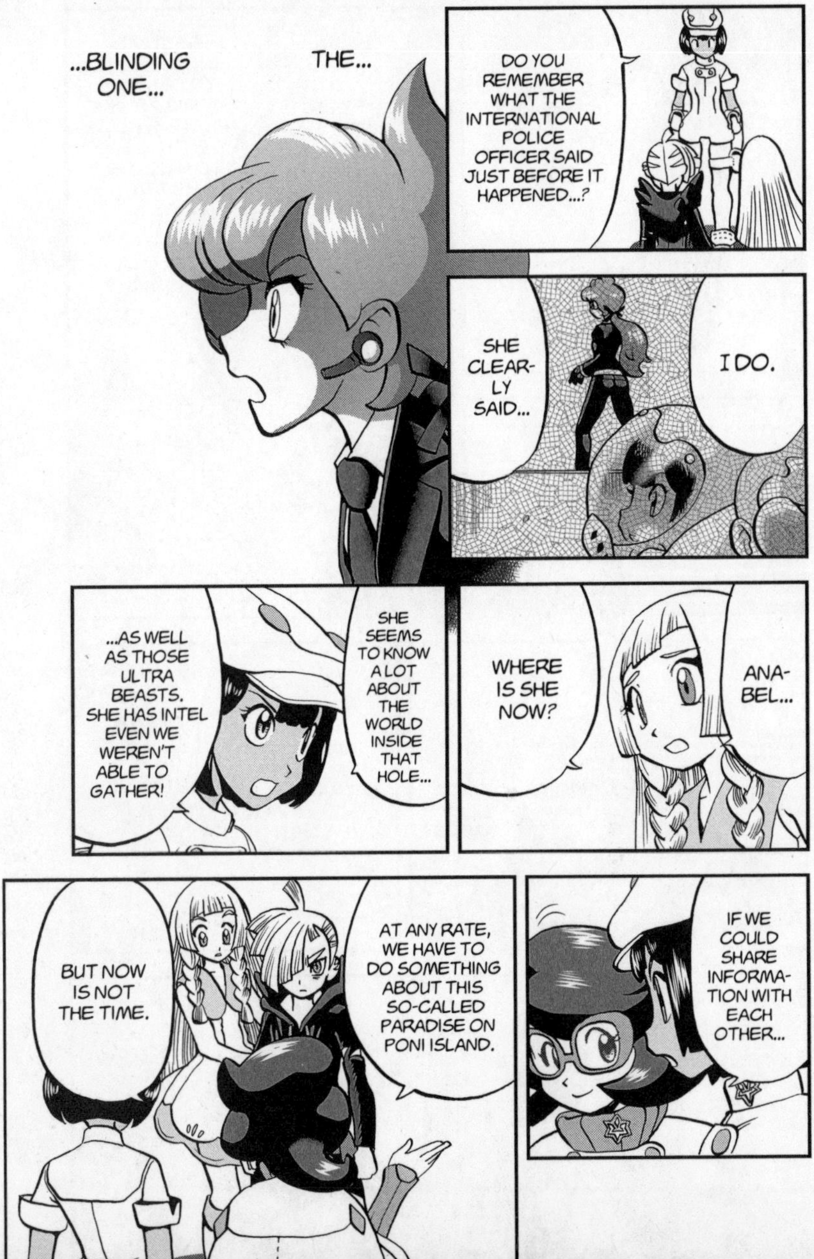
DO YOU REMEMBER WHAT THE INTERNATIONAL POLICE OFFICER SAID JUST BEFORE IT HAPPENED...?
I DO.
SHE CLEAR-LY SAID...
THE...
...BLINDING ONE...
ANA-BEL...
WHERE IS SHE NOW?
SHE SEEMS TO KNOW A LOT ABOUT THE WORLD INSIDE THAT HOLE...
...AS WELL AS THOSE ULTRA BEASTS. SHE HAS INTEL EVEN WE WEREN'T ABLE TO GATHER!
IF WE COULD SHARE INFORMA-TION WITH EACH OTHER...
AT ANY RATE, WE HAVE TO DO SOMETHING ABOUT THIS SO-CALLED PARADISE ON PONI ISLAND.
BUT NOW IS NOT THE TIME.

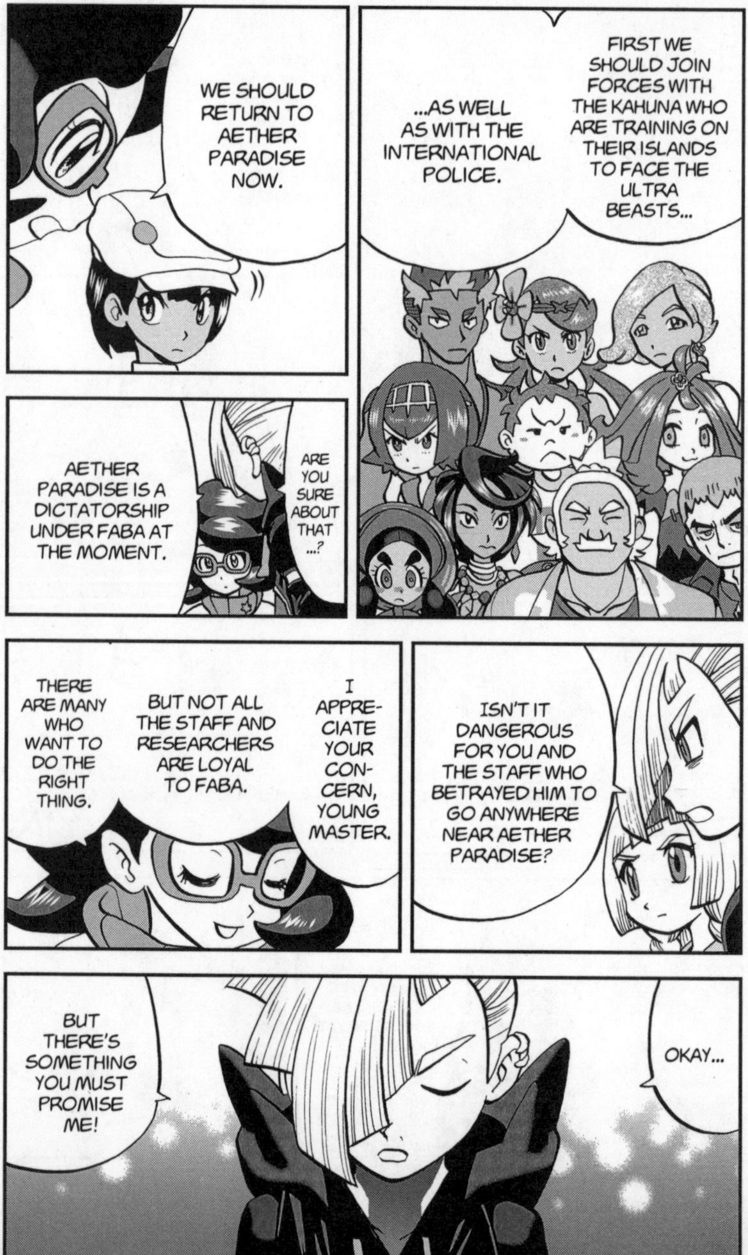
FIRST WE SHOULD JOIN FORCES WITH THE KAHUNA WHO ARE TRAINING ON THEIR ISLANDS TO FACE THE ULTRA BEASTS...
...AS WELL AS WITH THE INTERNATIONAL POLICE.
WE SHOULD RETURN TO AETHER PARADISE NOW.
ARE YOU SURE ABOUT THAT ...?
AETHER PARADISE IS A DICTATORSHIP UNDER FABA AT THE MOMENT.
ISN'T IT DANGEROUS FOR YOU AND THE STAFF WHO BETRAYED HIM TO GO ANYWHERE NEAR AETHER PARADISE?
I APPRE-CIATE YOUR CON-CERN, YOUNG MASTER.
BUT NOT ALL THE STAFF AND RESEARCHERS ARE LOYAL TO FABA.
THERE ARE MANY WHO WANT TO DO THE RIGHT THING.
OKAY...
BUT THERE'S SOMETHING YOU MUST PROMISE ME!

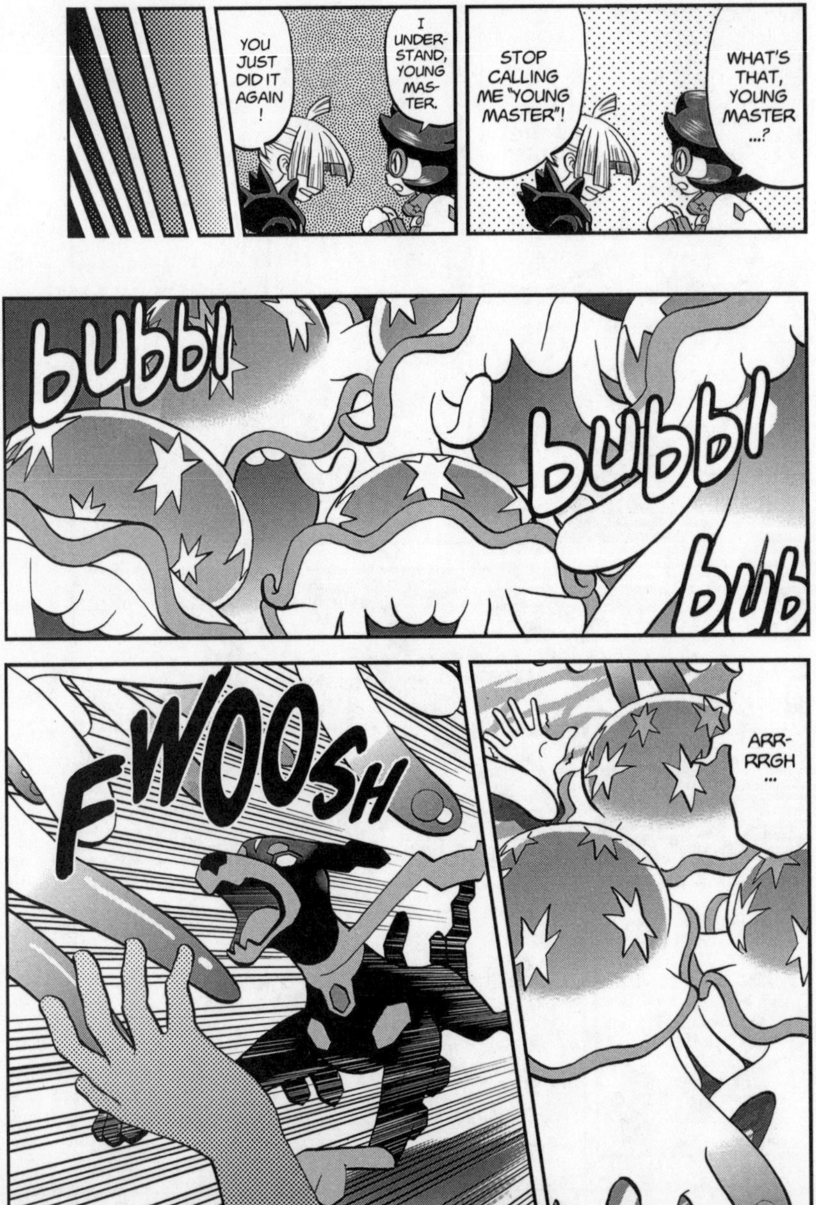
WHAT'S THAT, YOUNG MASTER ...?
STOP CALLING ME "YOUNG MASTER"!
I UNDER-STAND, YOUNG MAS-TER.
YOU JUST DID IT AGAIN !
bubbi
bubbi
bub
ARR-RRGH ...
FWOOSH

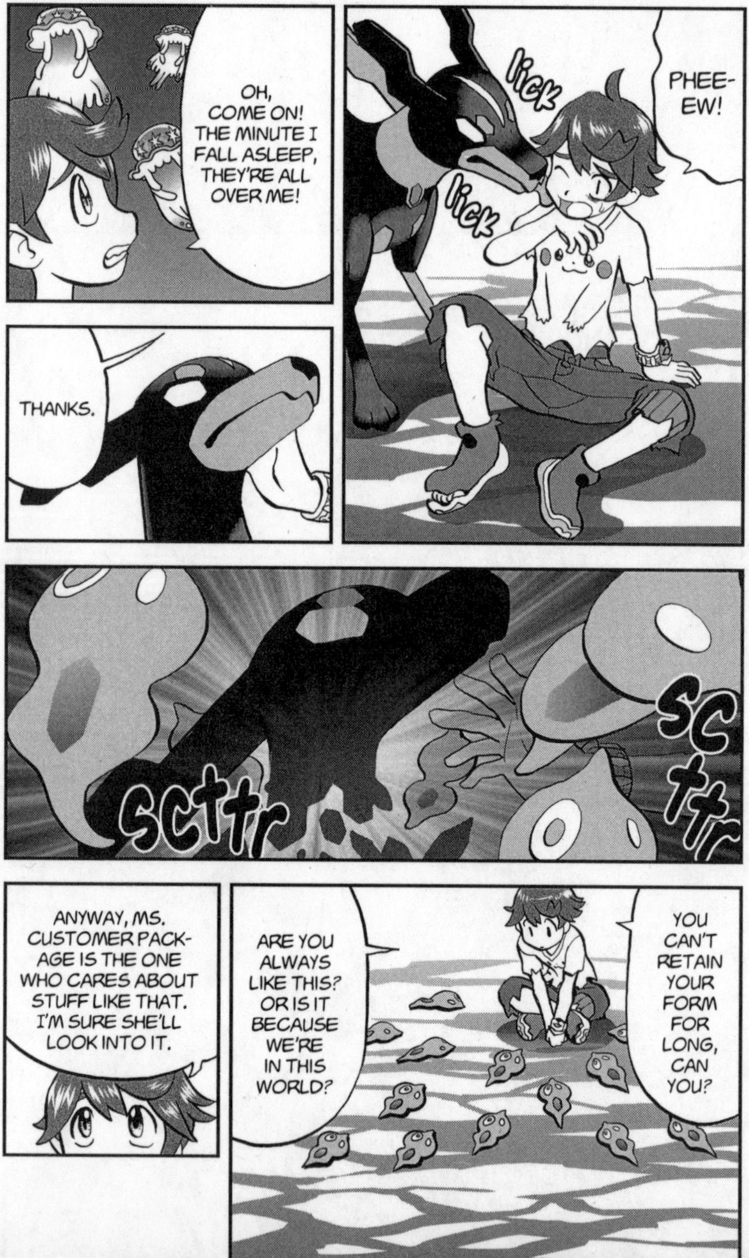
PHEE-EW!
lick
lick
OH, COME ON! THE MINUTE I FALL ASLEEP, THEY'RE ALL OVER ME!
THANKS.
scttr
scttr
YOU CAN'T RETAIN YOUR FORM FOR LONG, CAN YOU?
ARE YOU ALWAYS LIKE THIS? OR IS IT BECAUSE WE'RE IN THIS WORLD?
ANYWAY, MS. CUSTOMER PACKAGE IS THE ONE WHO CARES ABOUT STUFF LIKE THAT. I'M SURE SHE'LL LOOK INTO IT.

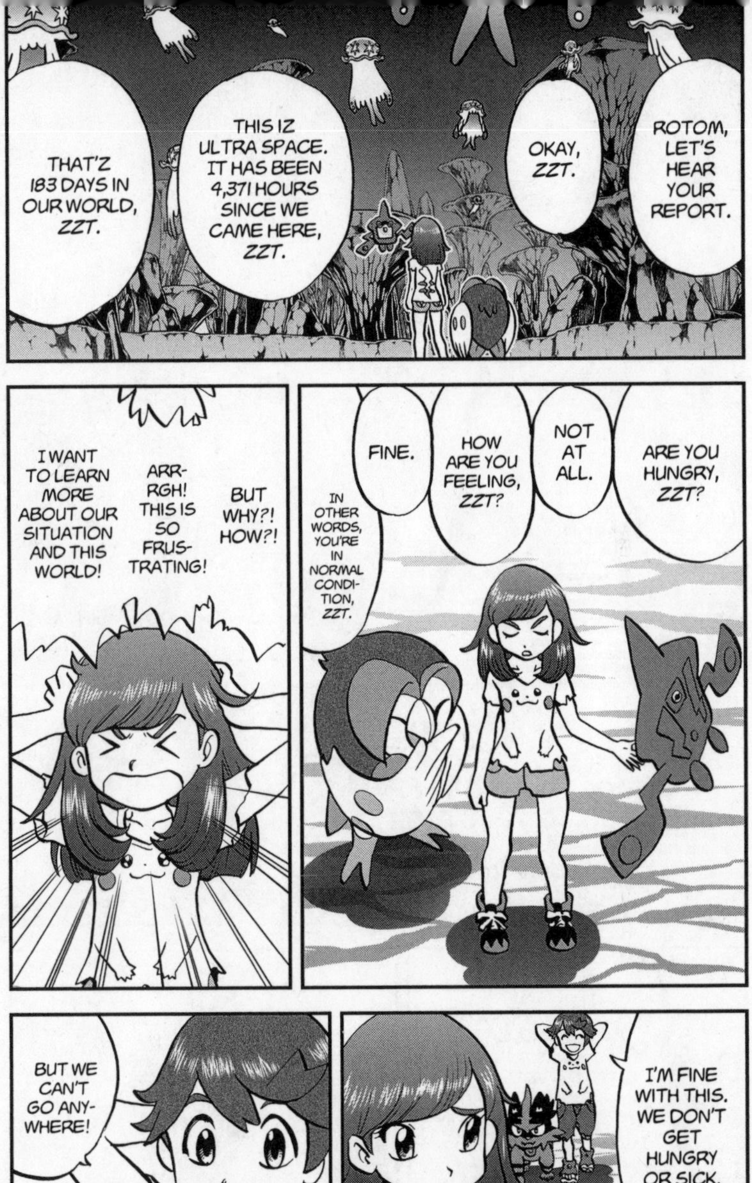
ROTOM, LET'S HEAR YOUR REPORT.
OKAY, ZZT.
THIS IZ ULTRA SPACE. IT HAS BEEN 4,371 HOURS SINCE WE CAME HERE, ZZT.
THAT'Z 183 DAYS IN OUR WORLD, ZZT.
ARE YOU HUNGRY, ZZT?
NOT AT ALL.
HOW ARE YOU FEELING, ZZT?
FINE.
IN OTHER WORDS, YOU'RE IN NORMAL CONDITION, ZZT.
BUT WHY?! HOW?!
ARRRGH! THIS IS SO FRUSTRATING!
I WANT TO LEARN MORE ABOUT OUR SITUATION AND THIS WORLD!
I'M FINE WITH THIS. WE DON'T GET HUNGRY OR SICK.
BUT WE CAN'T GO ANYWHERE!

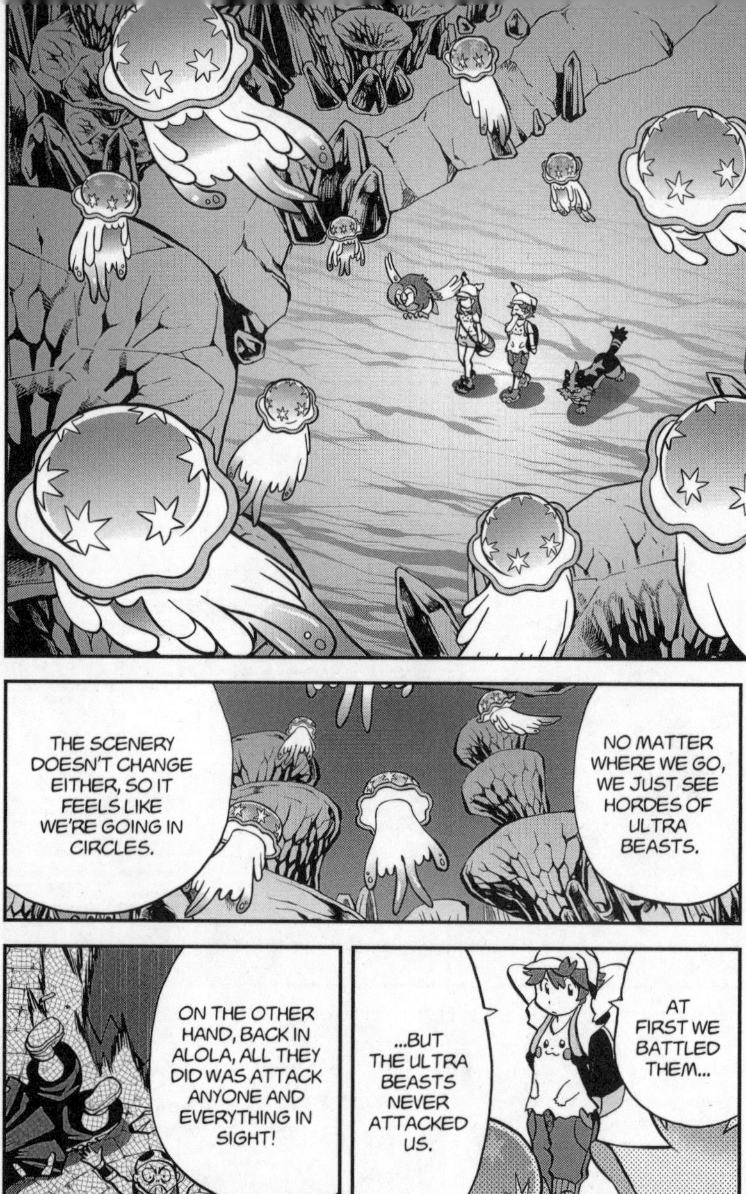
NO MATTER WHERE WE GO, WE JUST SEE HORDES OF ULTRA BEASTS.
THE SCENERY DOESN'T CHANGE EITHER, SO IT FEELS LIKE WE'RE GOING IN CIRCLES.
AT FIRST WE BATTLED THEM...
...BUT THE ULTRA BEASTS NEVER ATTACKED US.
ON THE OTHER HAND, BACK IN ALOLA, ALL THEY DID WAS ATTACK ANYONE AND EVERYTHING IN SIGHT!

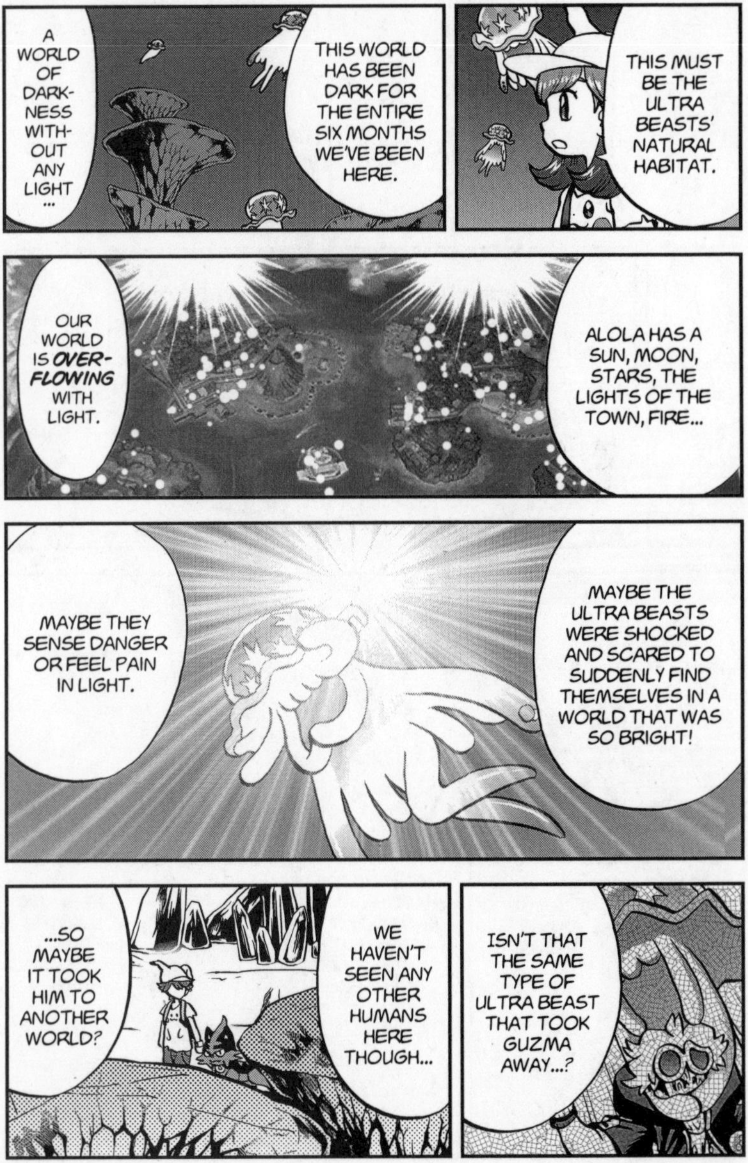
THIS MUST BE THE ULTRA BEASTS' NATURAL HABITAT.
THIS WORLD HAS BEEN DARK FOR THE ENTIRE SIX MONTHS WE'VE BEEN HERE.
A WORLD OF DARK-NESS WITH-OUT ANY LIGHT...
ALOLA HAS A SUN, MOON, STARS, THE LIGHTS OF THE TOWN, FIRE...
OUR WORLD IS ***OVER-FLOWING*** WITH LIGHT.
MAYBE THE ULTRA BEASTS WERE SHOCKED AND SCARED TO SUDDENLY FIND THEMSELVES IN A WORLD THAT WAS SO BRIGHT!
MAYBE THEY SENSE DANGER OR FEEL PAIN IN LIGHT.
ISN'T THAT THE SAME TYPE OF ULTRA BEAST THAT TOOK GUZMA AWAY...?
WE HAVEN'T SEEN ANY OTHER HUMANS HERE THOUGH...
...SO MAYBE IT TOOK HIM TO ANOTHER WORLD?

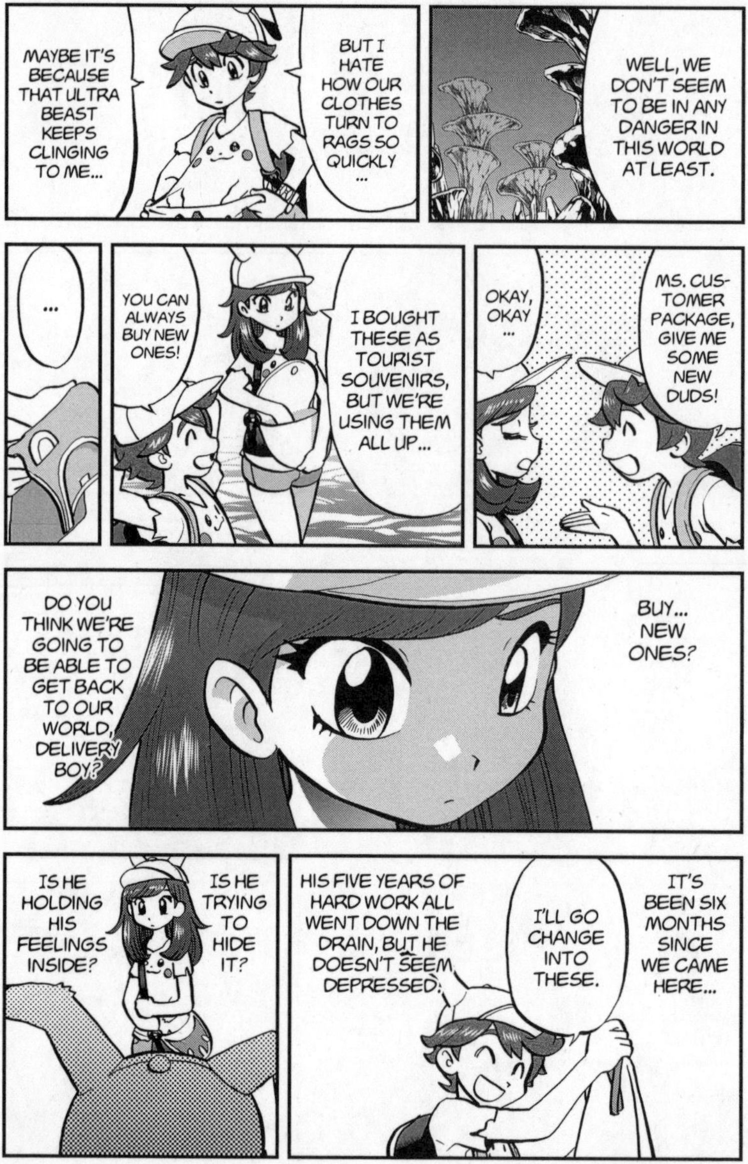
WELL, WE DON'T SEEM TO BE IN ANY DANGER IN THIS WORLD AT LEAST.
BUT I HATE HOW OUR CLOTHES TURN TO RAGS SO QUICKLY ...
MAYBE IT'S BECAUSE THAT ULTRA BEAST KEEPS CLINGING TO ME...
MS. CUS-TOMER PACKAGE, GIVE ME SOME NEW DUDS!
OKAY, OKAY ...
I BOUGHT THESE AS TOURIST SOUVENIRS, BUT WE'RE USING THEM ALL UP...
YOU CAN ALWAYS BUY NEW ONES!
...
BUY... NEW ONES?
DO YOU THINK WE'RE GOING TO BE ABLE TO GET BACK TO OUR WORLD, DELIVERY BOY?
IT'S BEEN SIX MONTHS SINCE WE CAME HERE...
I'LL GO CHANGE INTO THESE.
HIS FIVE YEARS OF HARD WORK ALL WENT DOWN THE DRAIN, BUT HE DOESN'T SEEM DEPRESSED.
IS HE TRYING TO HIDE IT?
IS HE HOLDING HIS FEELINGS INSIDE?

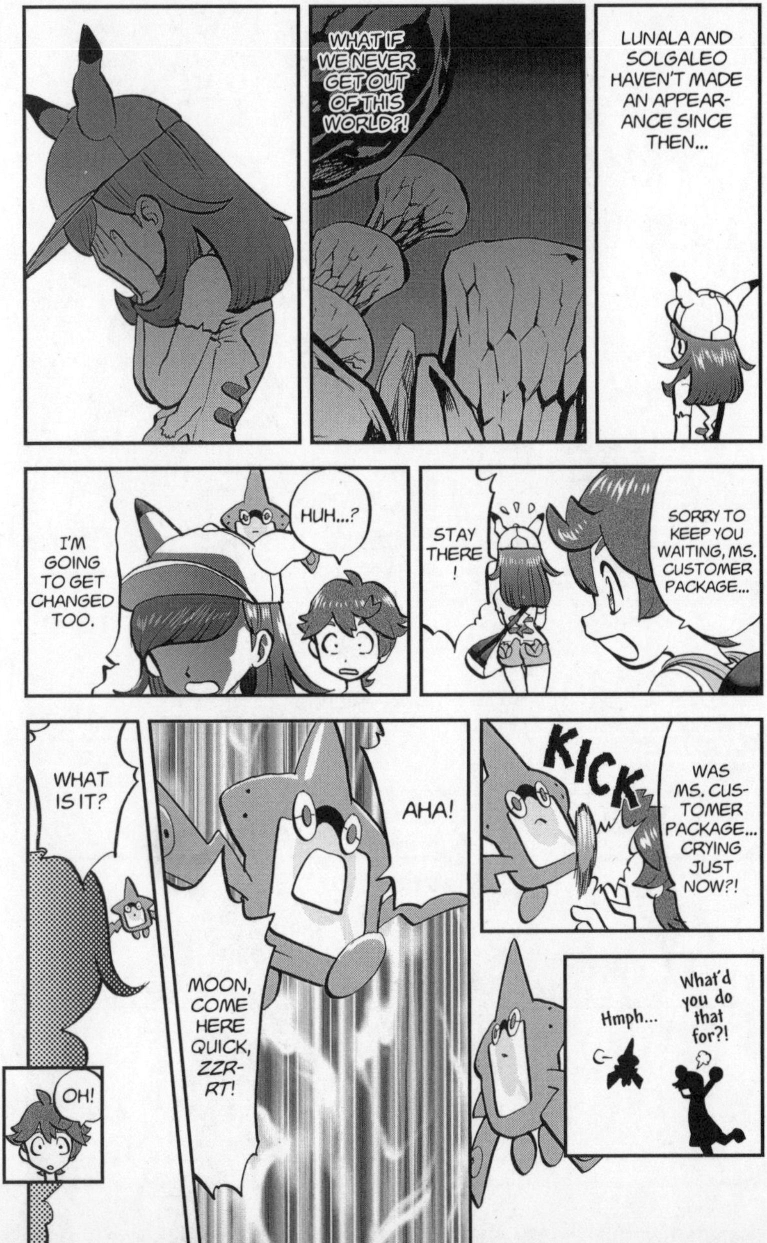
LUNALA AND SOLGALEO HAVEN'T MADE AN APPEARANCE SINCE THEN...
WHAT IF WE NEVER GET OUT OF THIS WORLD?!
SORRY TO KEEP YOU WAITING, MS. CUSTOMER PACKAGE...
STAY THERE!
I'M GOING TO GET CHANGED TOO.
HUH...?
WAS MS. CUSTOMER PACKAGE... CRYING JUST NOW?!
KICK
What'd you do that for?!
Hmph...
AHA!
MOON, COME HERE QUICK, ZZR-RT!
WHAT IS IT?
OH!

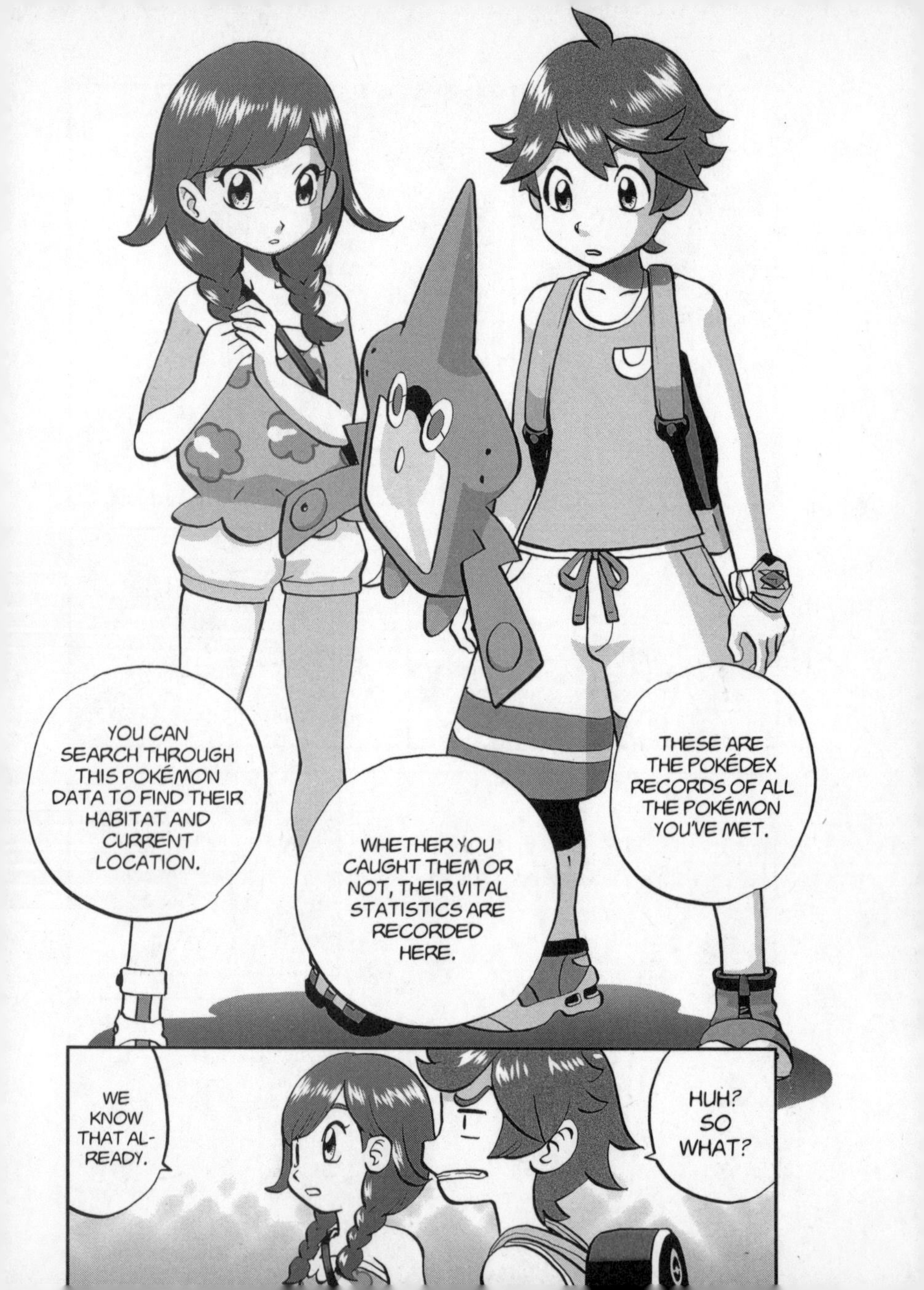
THESE ARE THE POKÉDEX RECORDS OF ALL THE POKÉMON YOU'VE MET.
WHETHER YOU CAUGHT THEM OR NOT, THEIR VITAL STATISTICS ARE RECORDED HERE.
YOU CAN SEARCH THROUGH THIS POKÉMON DATA TO FIND THEIR HABITAT AND CURRENT LOCATION.
HUH? SO WHAT?
WE KNOW THAT AL-READY.

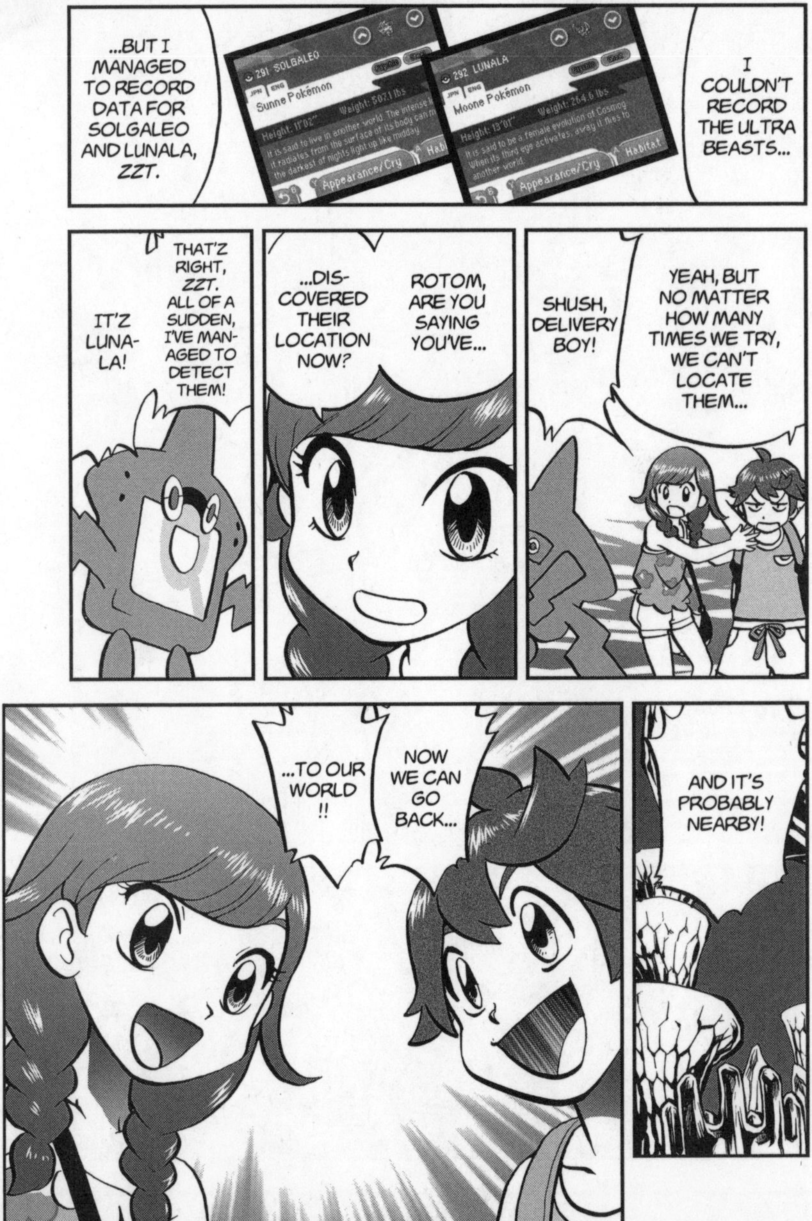
I COULDN'T RECORD THE ULTRA BEASTS...
291 SOLGALEO
Sunne Pokémon
Appearance/Cry
292 LUNALA
Moone Pokémon
Appearance/Cry
...BUT I MANAGED TO RECORD DATA FOR SOLGALEO AND LUNALA, ZZT.
YEAH, BUT NO MATTER HOW MANY TIMES WE TRY, WE CAN'T LOCATE THEM...
SHUSH, DELIVERY BOY!
ROTOM, ARE YOU SAYING YOU'VE...
...DIS-COVERED THEIR LOCATION NOW?
THAT'Z RIGHT, ZZT. ALL OF A SUDDEN, I'VE MAN-AGED TO DETECT THEM!
IT'Z LUNA-LA!
AND IT'S PROBABLY NEARBY!
NOW WE CAN GO BACK...
...TO OUR WORLD !!

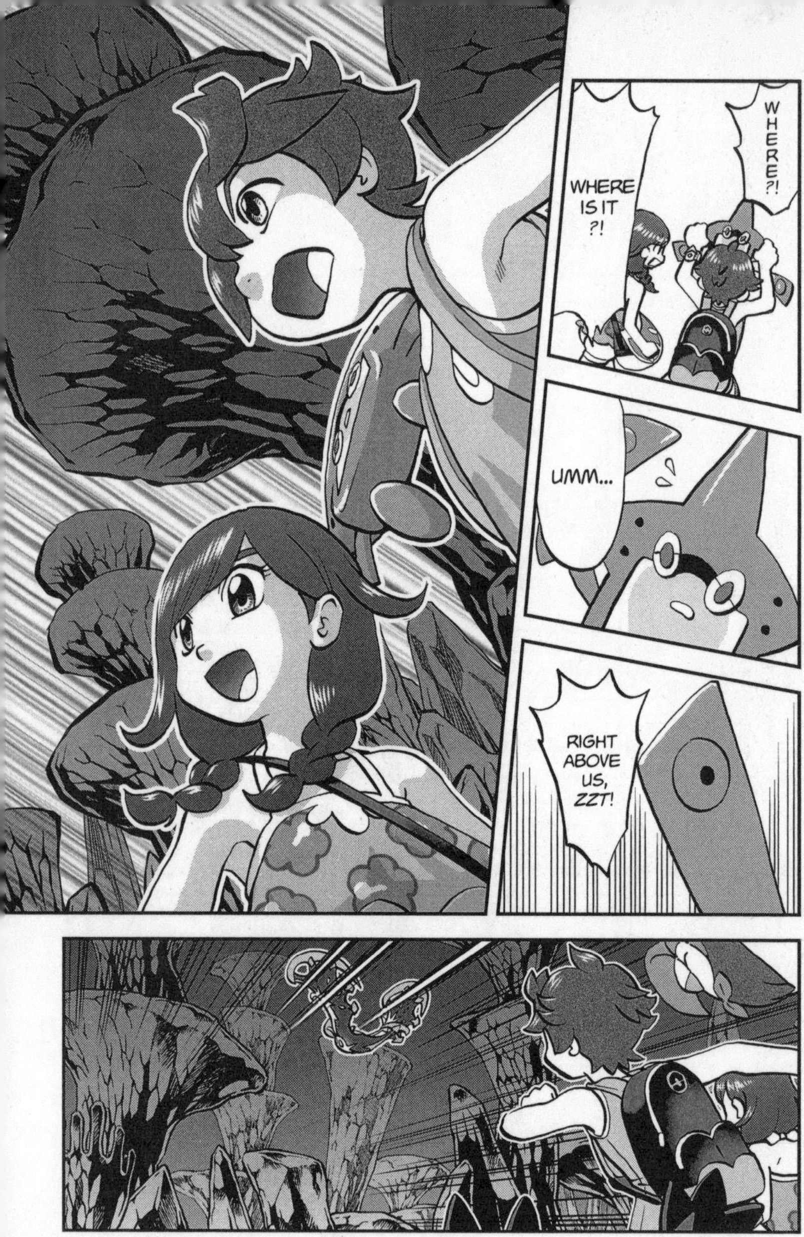
WHERE?!
WHERE IS IT ?!
UMM...
RIGHT ABOVE US, ZZT!

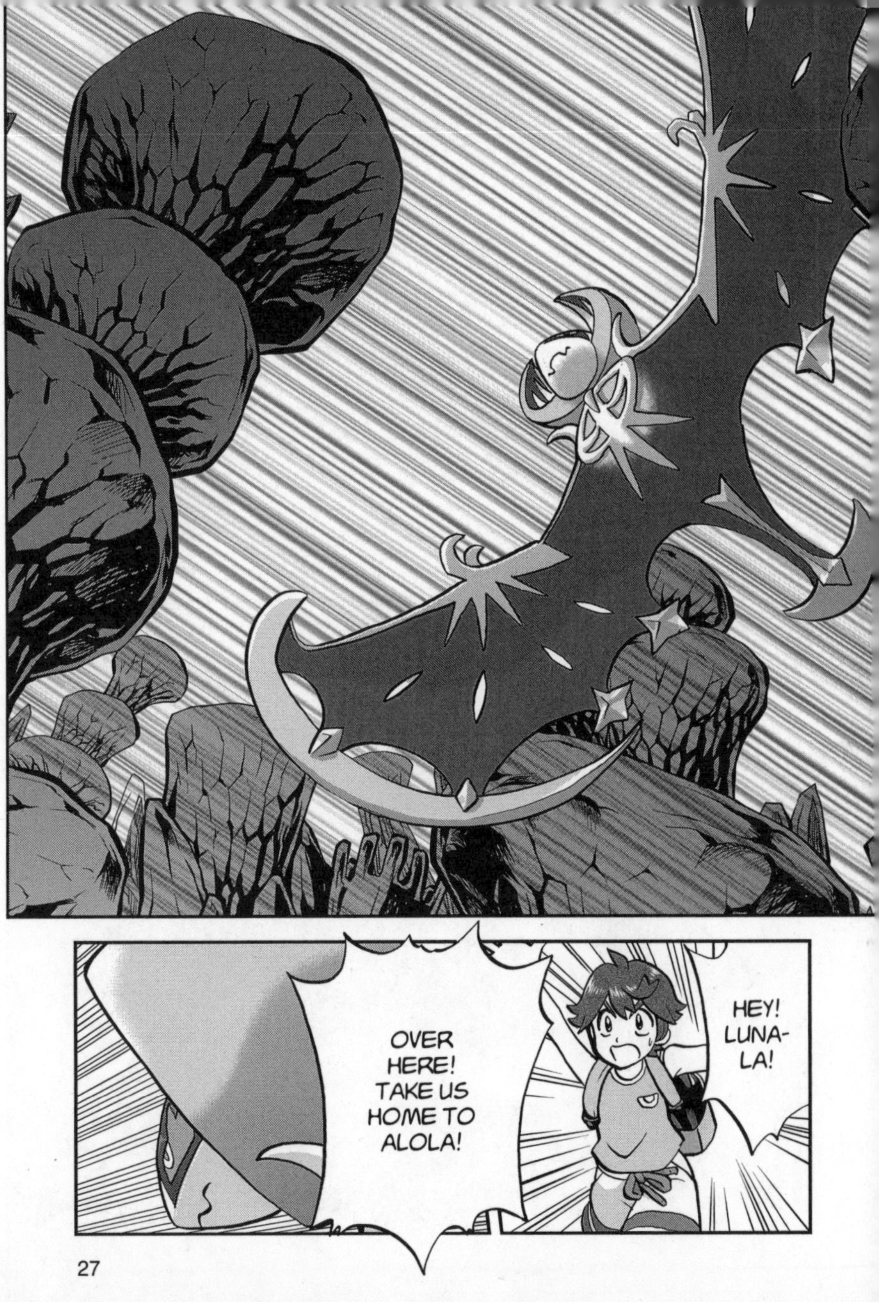
HEY! LUNA-LA!
OVER HERE! TAKE US HOME TO ALOLA!

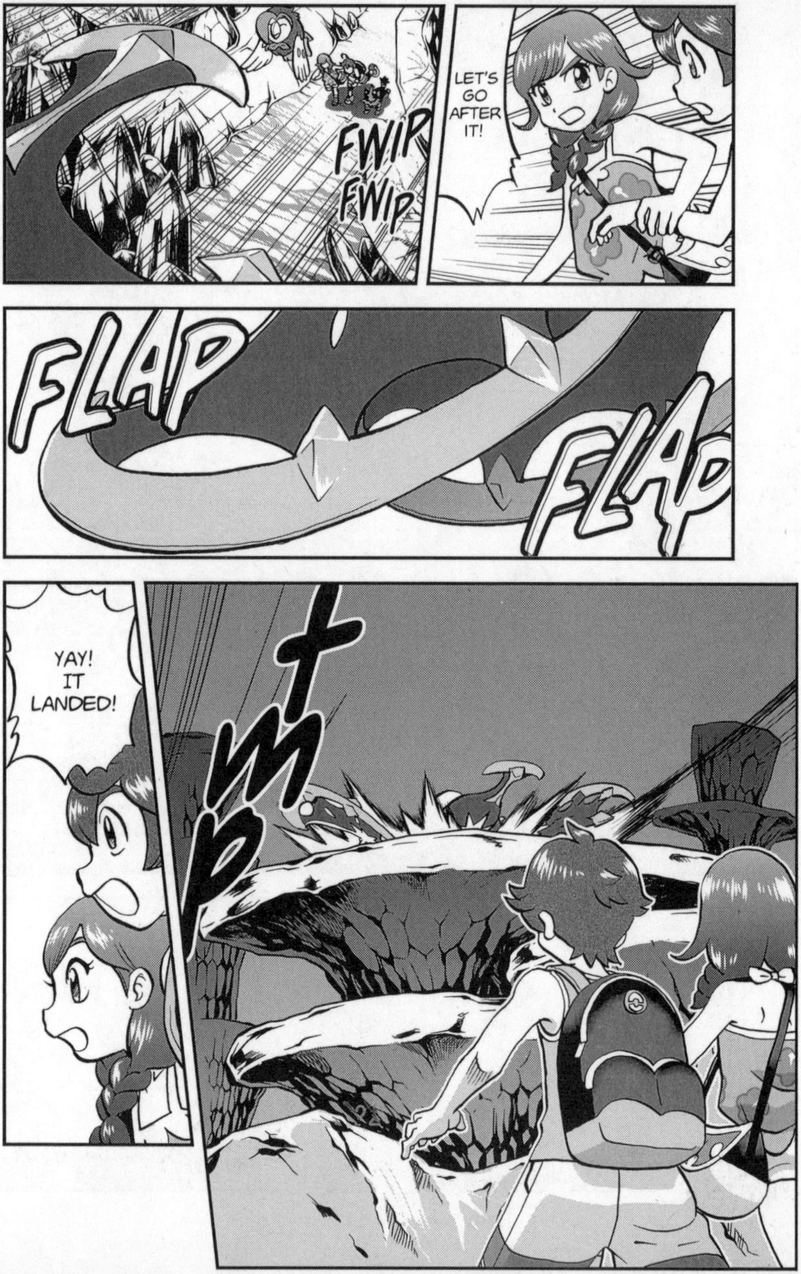

LET'S GO AFTER IT!
FWIP FWIP
FLAP
FLAP
YAY! IT LANDED!

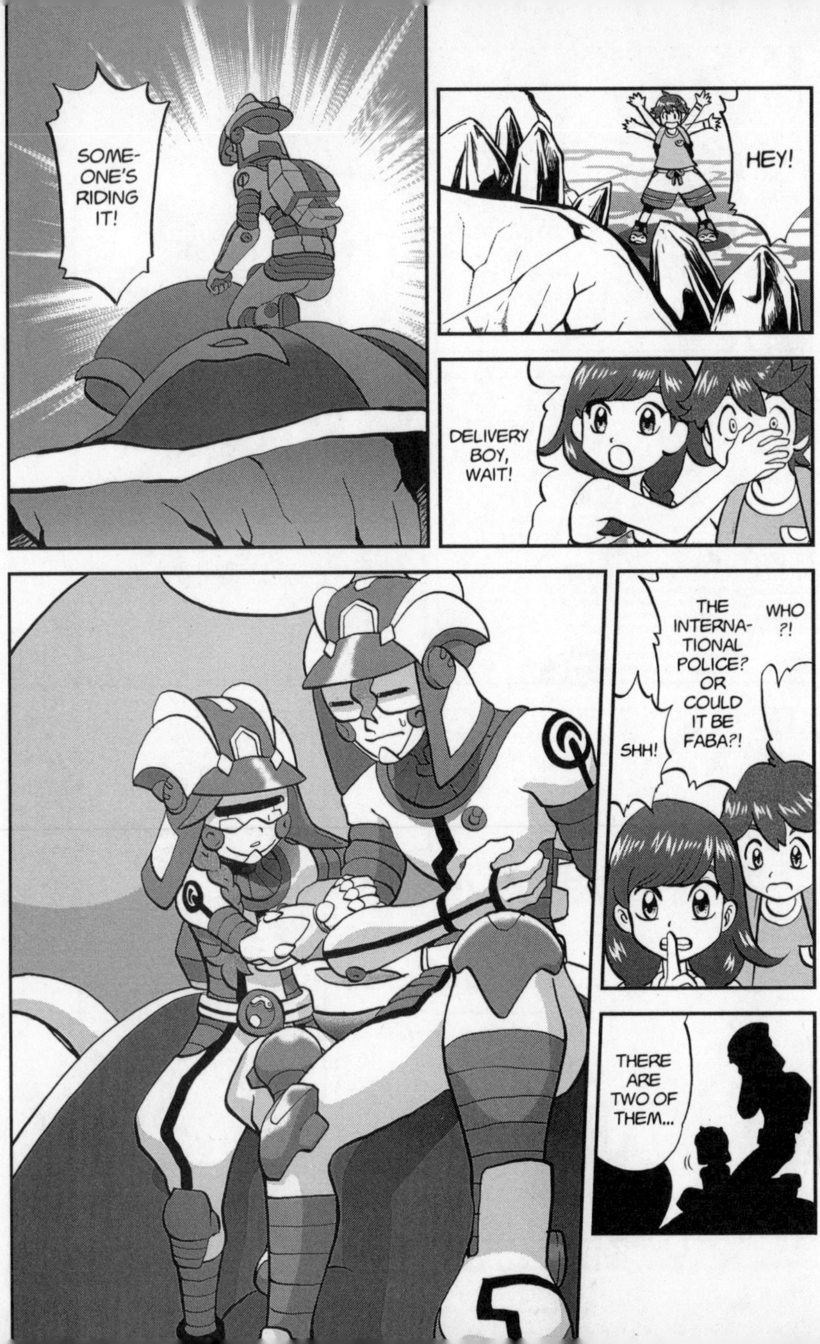
HEY!
DELIVERY BOY, WAIT!
SOME-ONE'S RIDING IT!
WHO ?!
THE INTERNA-TIONAL POLICE? OR COULD IT BE FABA?!
SHH!
THERE ARE TWO OF THEM...

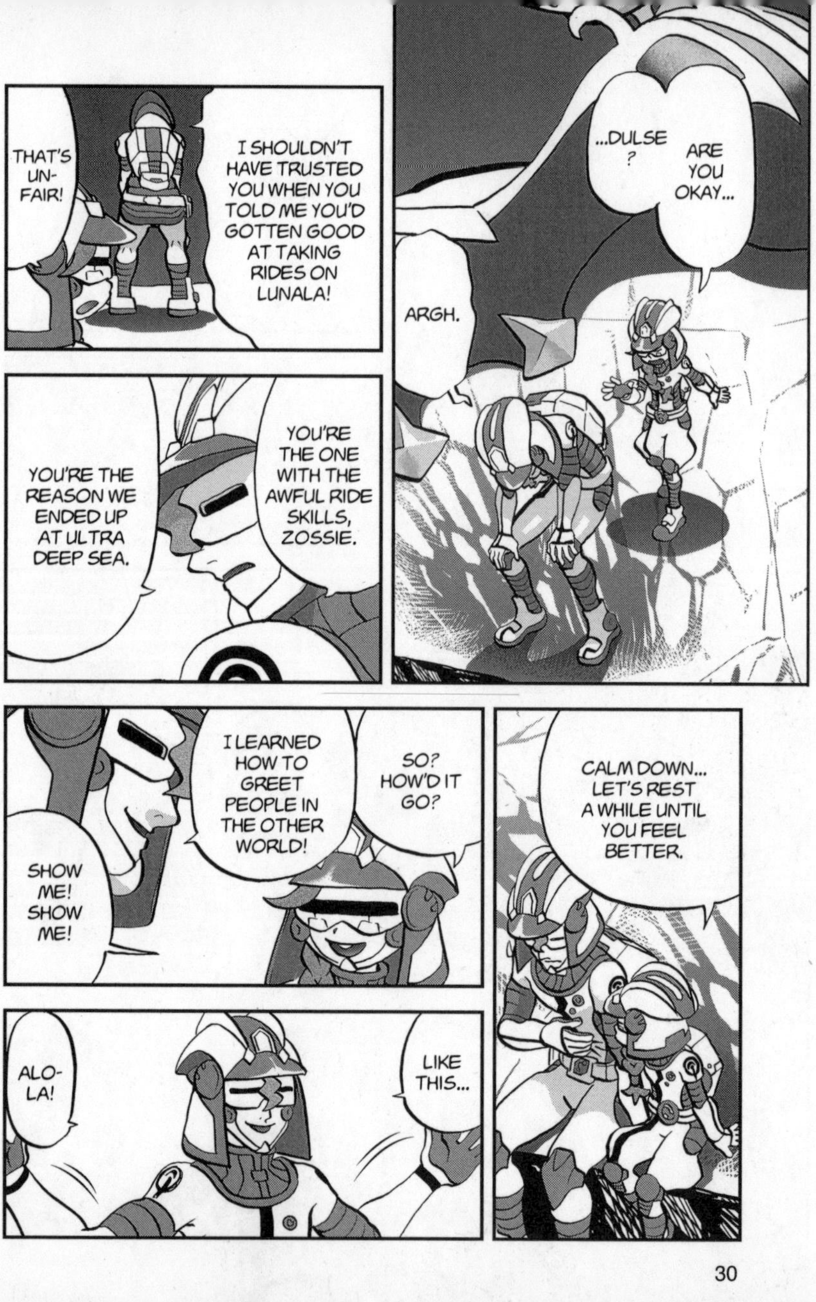
...DULSE? ARE YOU OKAY...
ARGH.
I SHOULDN'T HAVE TRUSTED YOU WHEN YOU TOLD ME YOU'D GOTTEN GOOD AT TAKING RIDES ON LUNALA!
THAT'S UN-FAIR!
YOU'RE THE ONE WITH THE AWFUL RIDE SKILLS, ZOSSIE.
YOU'RE THE REASON WE ENDED UP AT ULTRA DEEP SEA.
CALM DOWN... LET'S REST A WHILE UNTIL YOU FEEL BETTER.
SO? HOW'D IT GO?
I LEARNED HOW TO GREET PEOPLE IN THE OTHER WORLD!
SHOW ME! SHOW ME!
LIKE THIS...
ALO-LA!

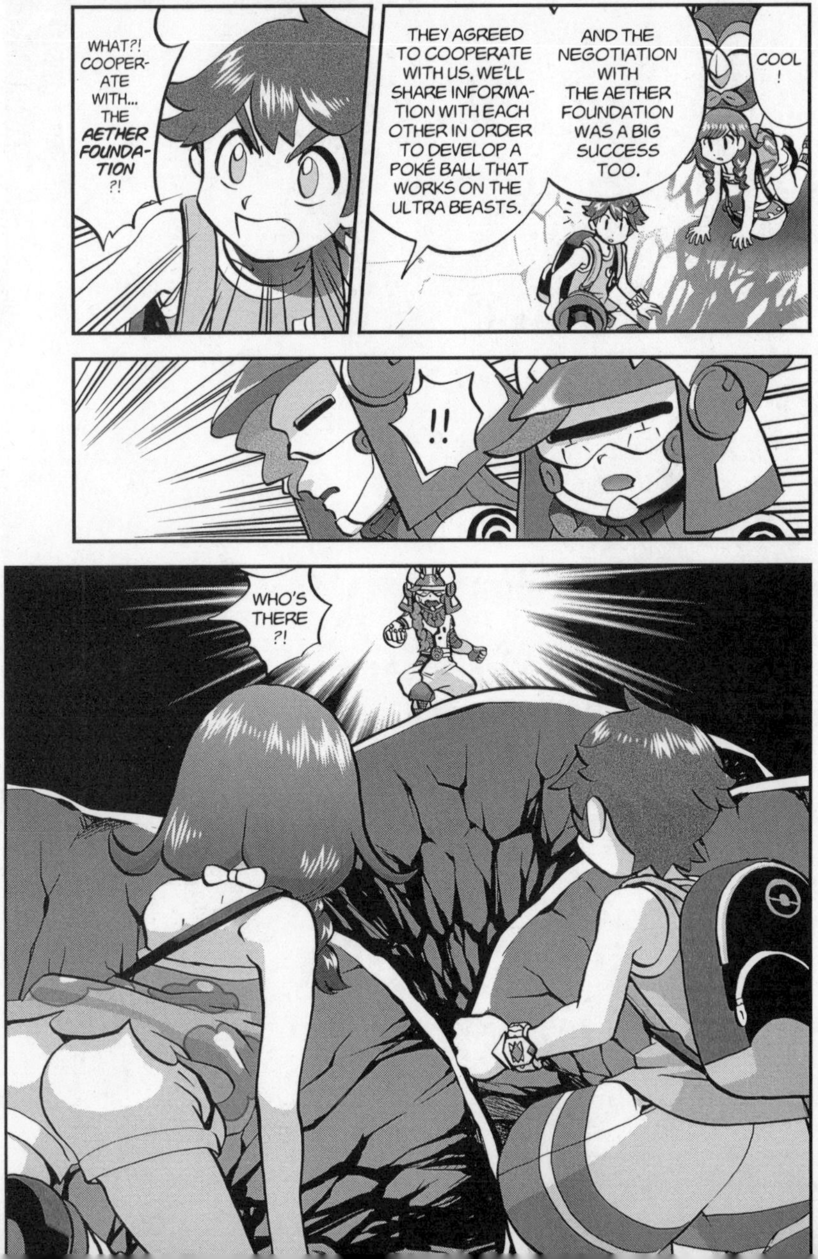
COOL!
AND THE NEGOTIATION WITH THE AETHER FOUNDATION WAS A BIG SUCCESS TOO.
THEY AGREED TO COOPERATE WITH US. WE'LL SHARE INFORMATION WITH EACH OTHER IN ORDER TO DEVELOP A POKÉ BALL THAT WORKS ON THE ULTRA BEASTS.
WHAT?! COOPERATE WITH... THE *AETHER FOUNDATION* ?!
!!
WHO'S THERE ?!

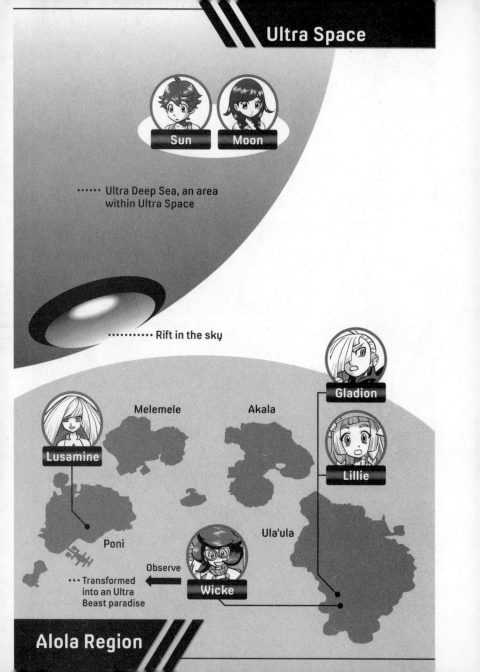

Sun

Moon

•••••• Ultra Deep Sea, an area
within Ultra Space

••••••••••• Rift in the sky

Gladion

Lusamine

Melemele

Akala

Lillie

Poni

Ula'ula

Observe

••• Transformed
into an Ultra
Beast paradise

Wicke

Alola Region

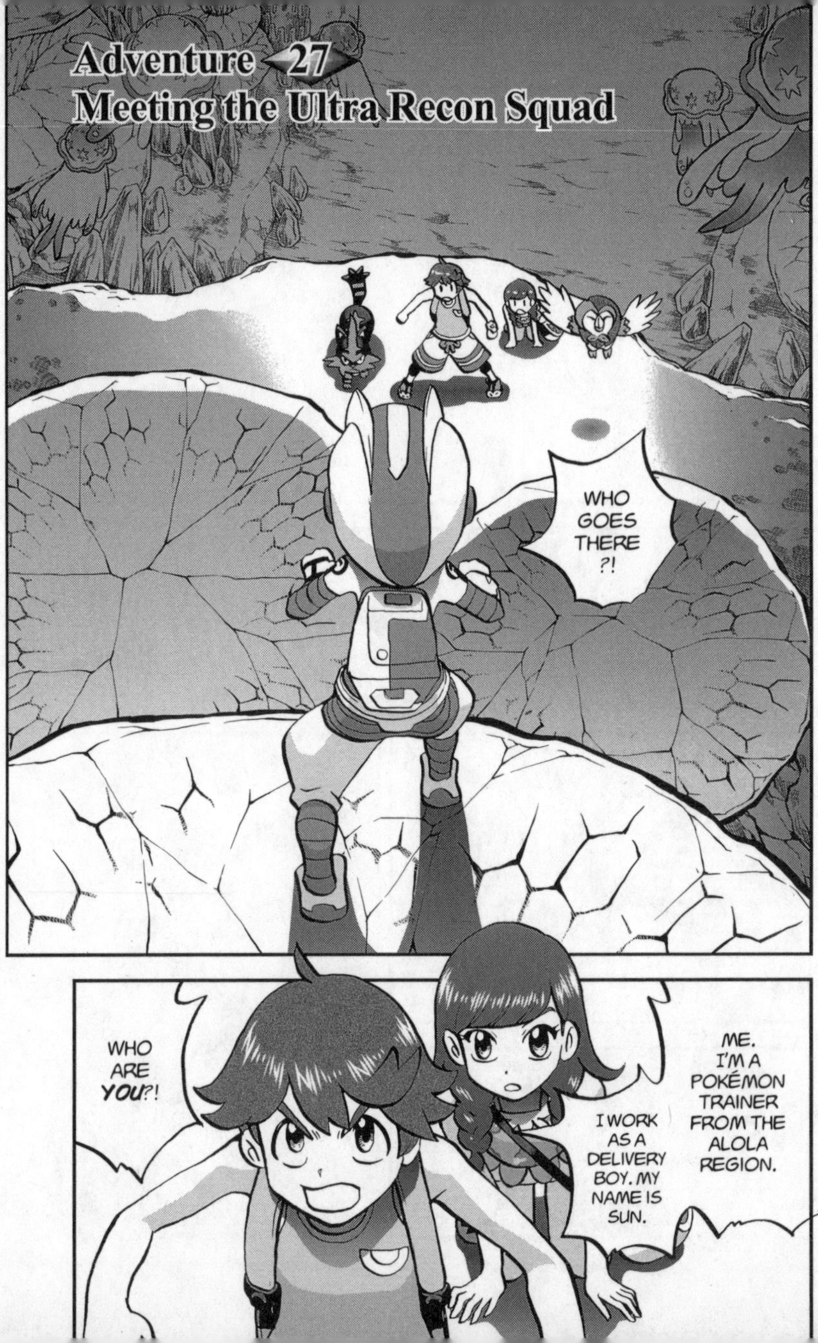
Adventure 27
Meeting the Ultra Recon Squad
WHO GOES THERE ?!
ME. I'M A POKÉMON TRAINER FROM THE ALOLA REGION.
I WORK AS A DELIVERY BOY. MY NAME IS SUN.
WHO ARE *YOU*?!

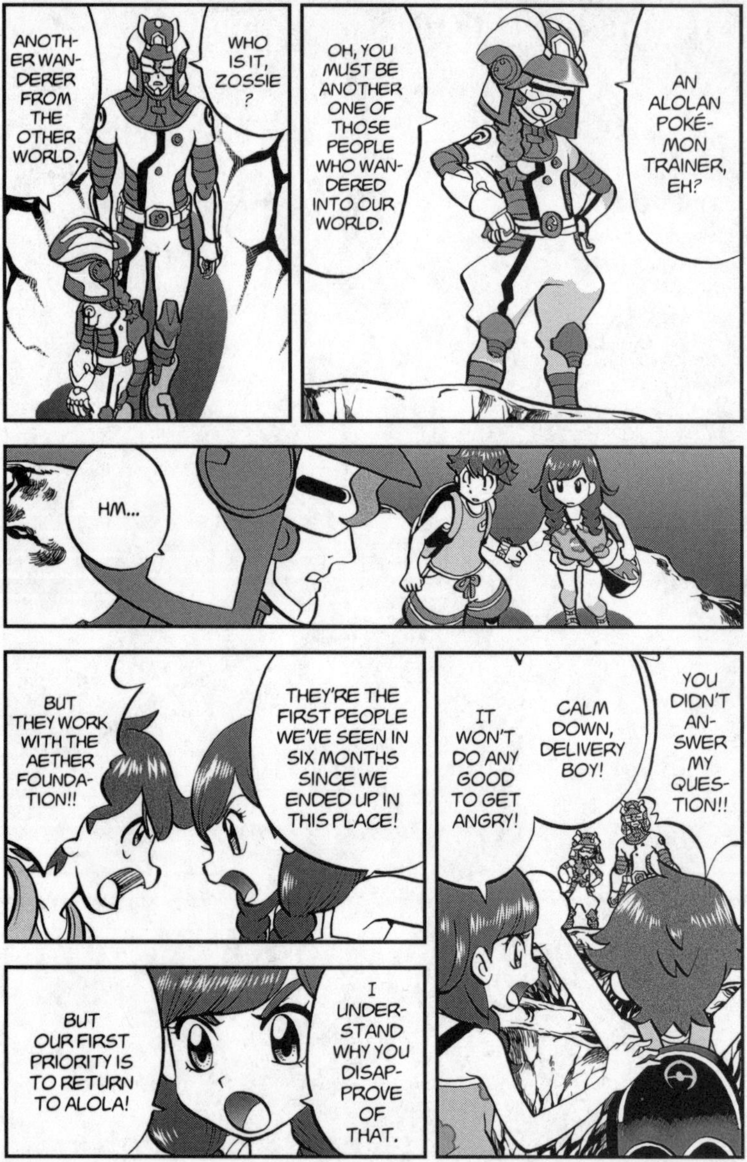
AN ALOLAN POKÉMON TRAINER, EH?
OH, YOU MUST BE ANOTHER ONE OF THOSE PEOPLE WHO WANDERED INTO OUR WORLD.
WHO IS IT, ZOSSIE?
ANOTHER WANDERER FROM THE OTHER WORLD.
HM...
YOU DIDN'T ANSWER MY QUESTION!!
CALM DOWN, DELIVERY BOY!
IT WON'T DO ANY GOOD TO GET ANGRY!
THEY'RE THE FIRST PEOPLE WE'VE SEEN IN SIX MONTHS SINCE WE ENDED UP IN THIS PLACE!
BUT THEY WORK WITH THE AETHER FOUNDATION!!
I UNDERSTAND WHY YOU DISAPPROVE OF THAT.
BUT OUR FIRST PRIORITY IS TO RETURN TO ALOLA!

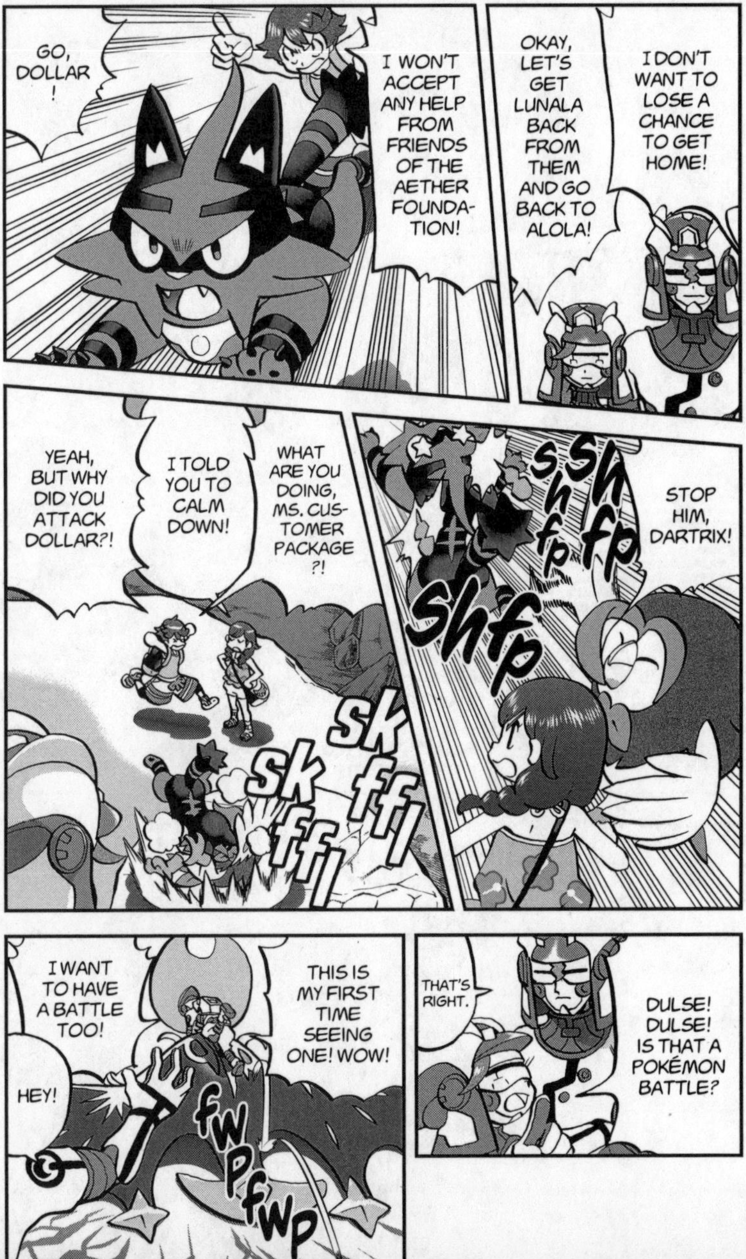

I DON'T WANT TO LOSE A CHANCE TO GET HOME!
OKAY, LET'S GET LUNALA BACK FROM THEM AND GO BACK TO ALOLA!
I WON'T ACCEPT ANY HELP FROM FRIENDS OF THE AETHER FOUNDATION!
GO, DOLLAR!
STOP HIM, DARTRIX!
shfp shfp shfp shfp
WHAT ARE YOU DOING, MS. CUSTOMER PACKAGE?!
I TOLD YOU TO CALM DOWN!
YEAH, BUT WHY DID YOU ATTACK DOLLAR?!
sk sk ffl ffl
DULSE! DULSE! IS THAT A POKÉMON BATTLE?
THAT'S RIGHT.
THIS IS MY FIRST TIME SEEING ONE! WOW!
I WANT TO HAVE A BATTLE TOO!
HEY!
fwp fwp

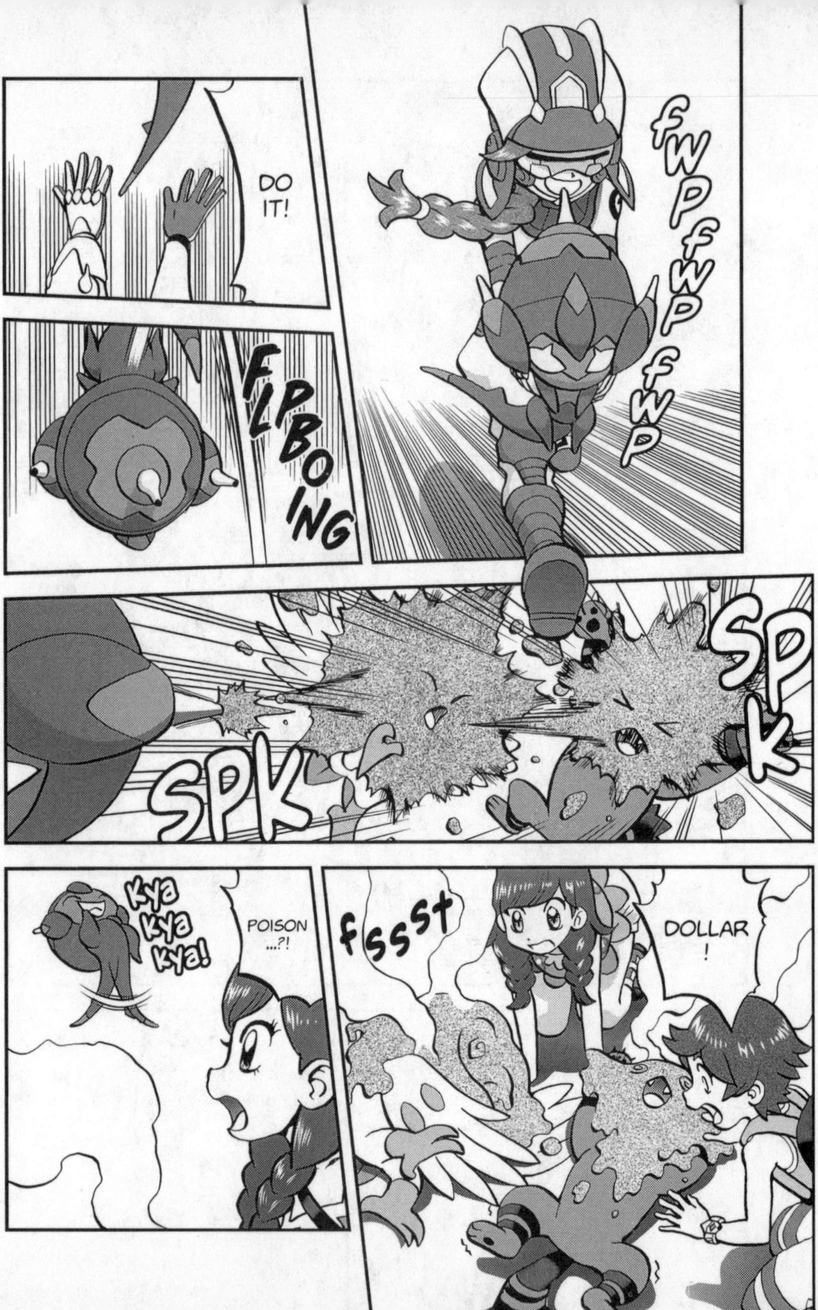
fwp fwp fwp fwp
DO IT!
FLPBOING
SPK
SPK
DOLLAR!
fssst
POISON...?!
Kya kya kya!

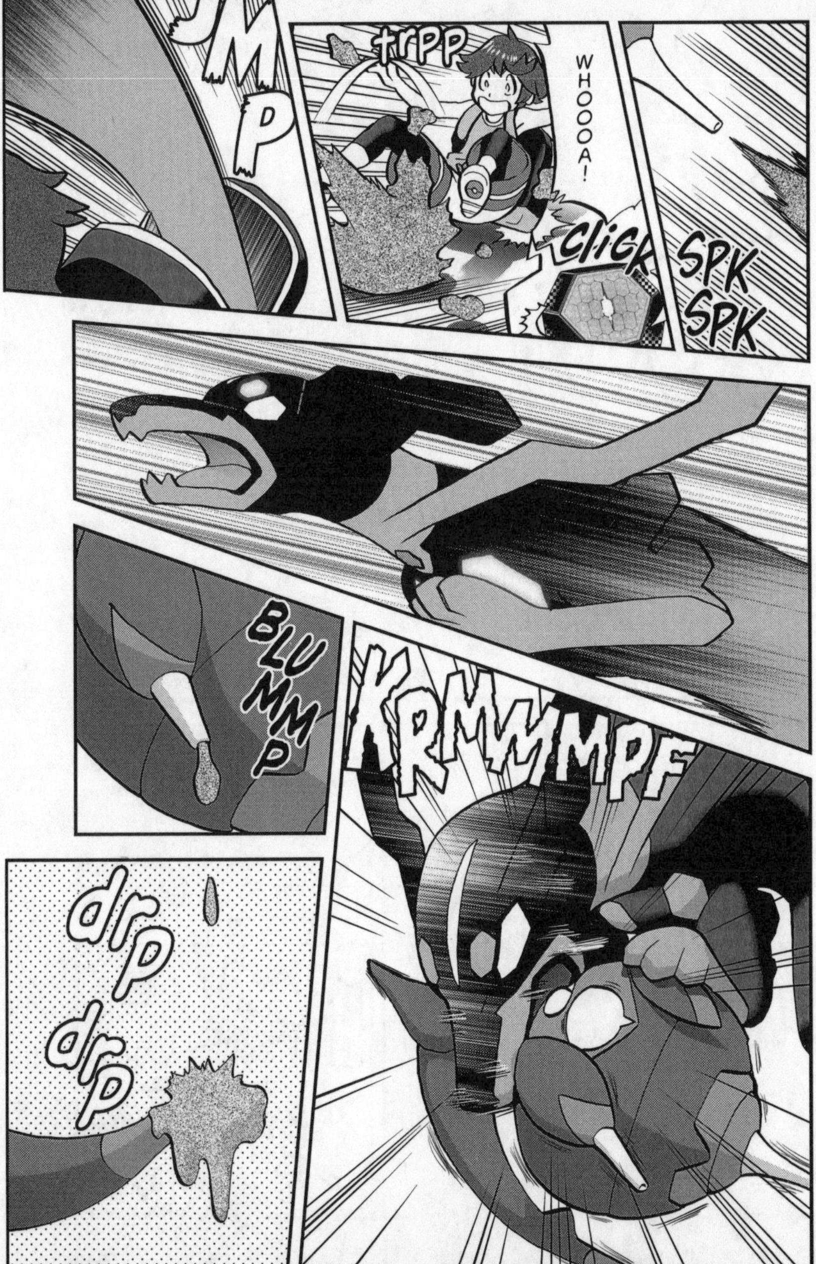
SPK
SPK
trpp
WHOOOOA!
Click
JMP
KRMMMPF
BLUMMMP
drp
drp

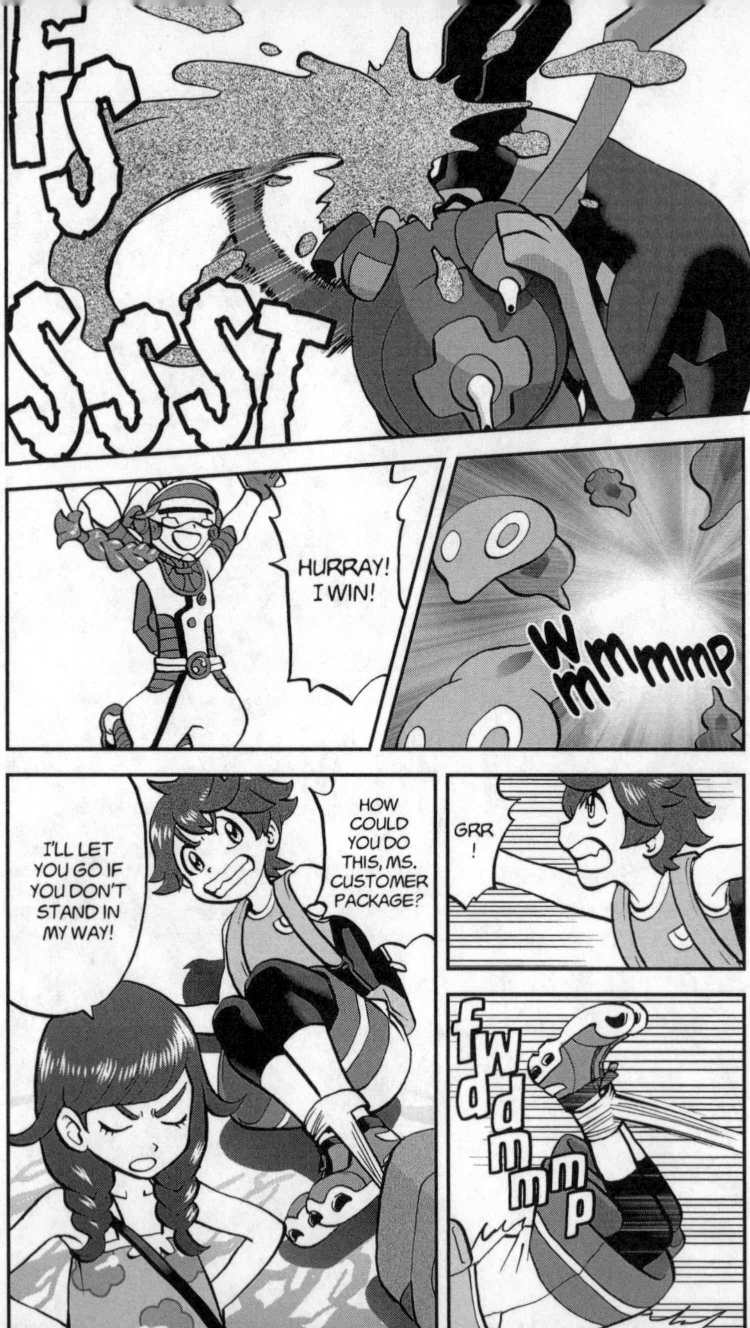
FSSSST
WMMMMP
HURRAY! I WIN!
GRR!
fwddmmmmp
HOW COULD YOU DO THIS, MS. CUSTOMER PACKAGE?
I'LL LET YOU GO IF YOU DON'T STAND IN MY WAY!

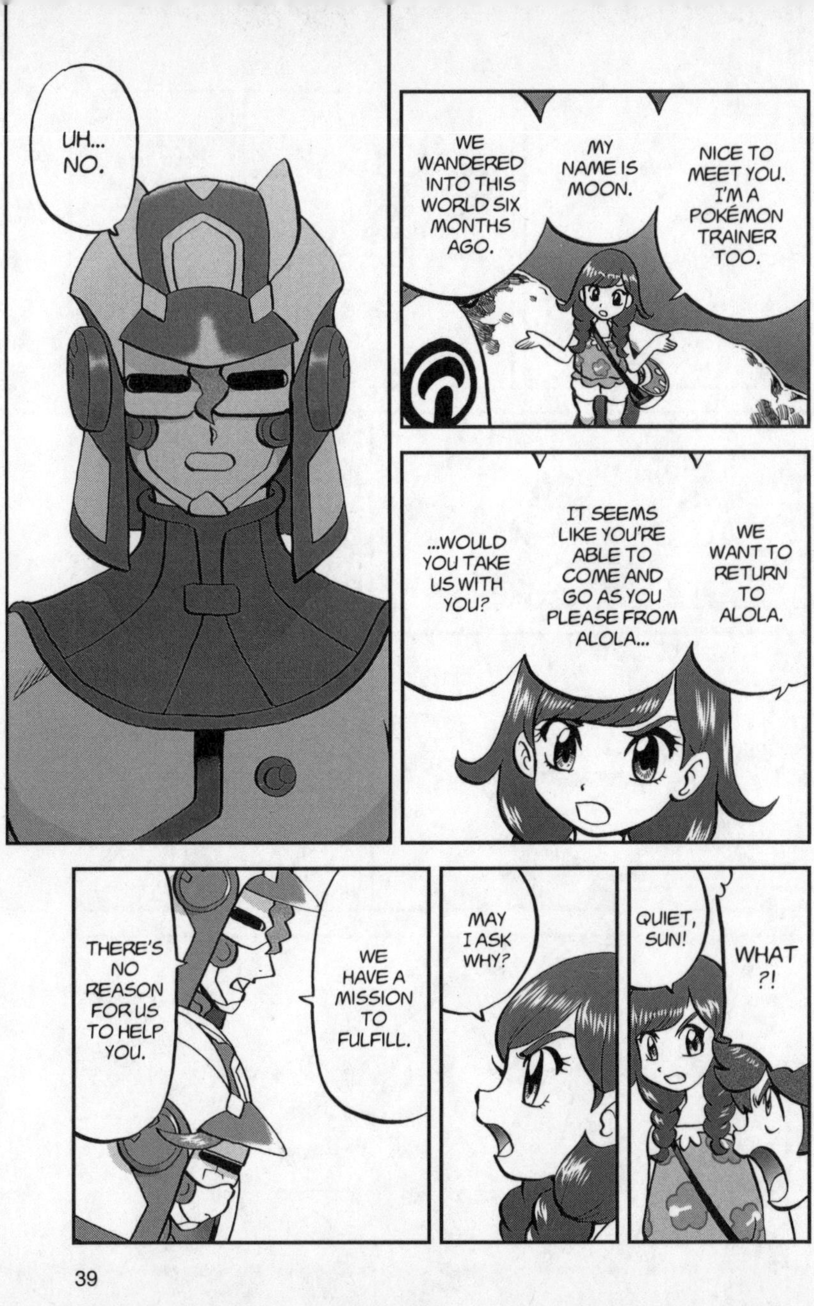
NICE TO MEET YOU. I'M A POKÉMON TRAINER TOO.
MY NAME IS MOON.
WE WANDERED INTO THIS WORLD SIX MONTHS AGO.
WE WANT TO RETURN TO ALOLA.
IT SEEMS LIKE YOU'RE ABLE TO COME AND GO AS YOU PLEASE FROM ALOLA...
...WOULD YOU TAKE US WITH YOU?
UH... NO.
WHAT ?!
QUIET, SUN!
MAY I ASK WHY?
WE HAVE A MISSION TO FULFILL.
THERE'S NO REASON FOR US TO HELP YOU.

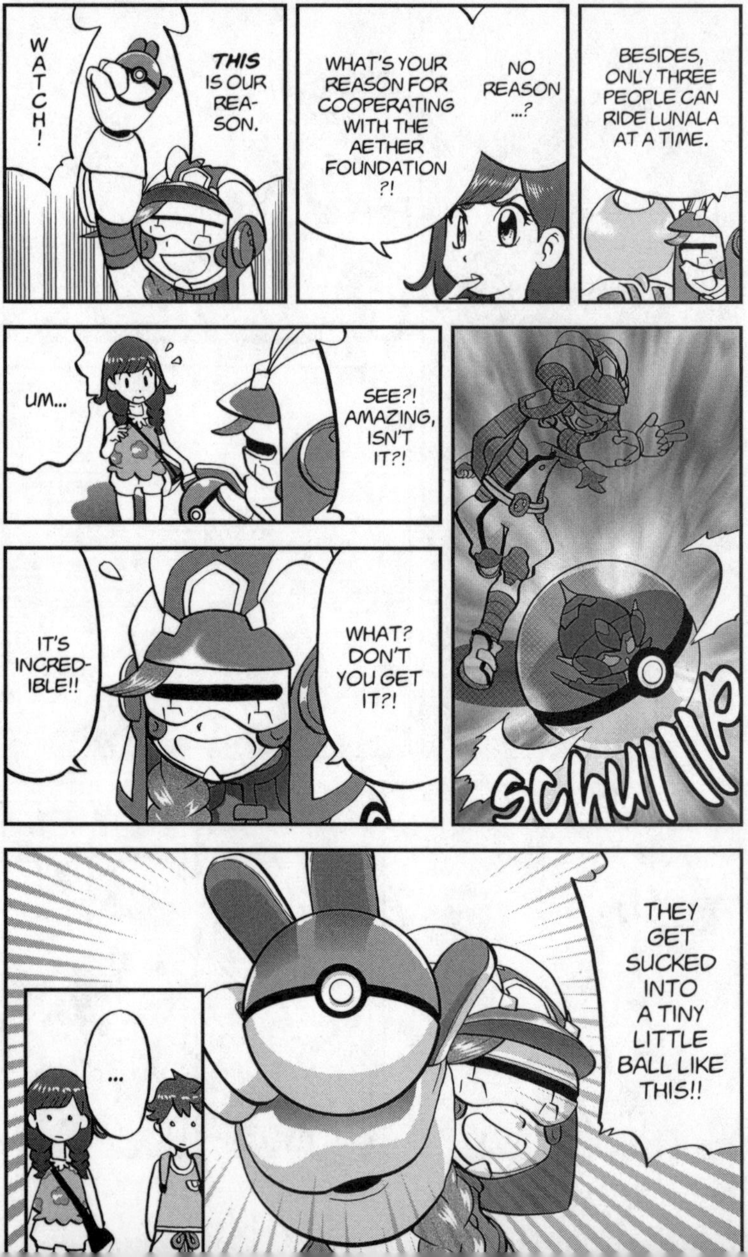
BESIDES, ONLY THREE PEOPLE CAN RIDE LUNALA AT A TIME.
NO REASON ...?
WHAT'S YOUR REASON FOR COOPERATING WITH THE AETHER FOUNDATION ?!
THIS IS OUR REA-SON.
WATCH!
SCHUUUP
SEE?! AMAZING, ISN'T IT?!
UM...
WHAT? DON'T YOU GET IT?!
IT'S INCRED-IBLE!!
THEY GET SUCKED INTO A TINY LITTLE BALL LIKE THIS!!
...

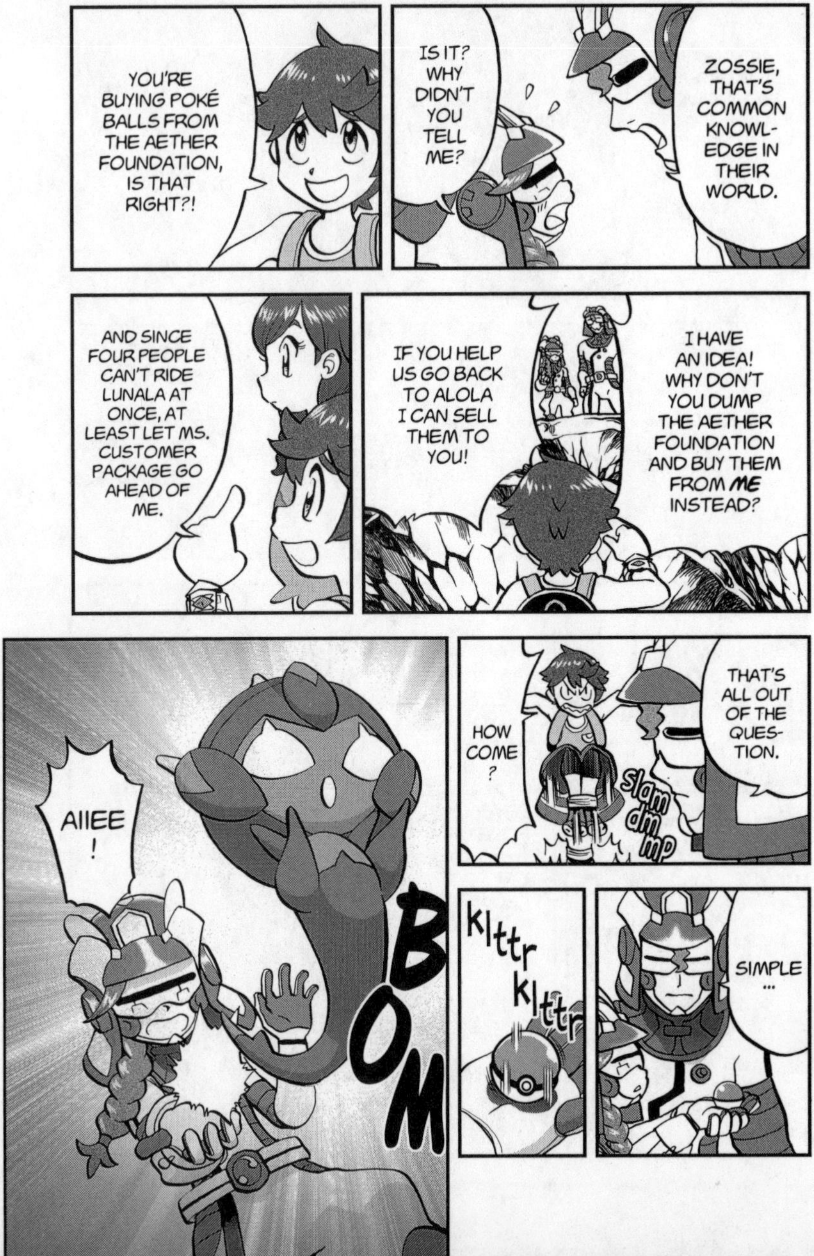
ZOSSIE, THAT'S COMMON KNOWL-EDGE IN THEIR WORLD.
IS IT? WHY DIDN'T YOU TELL ME?
YOU'RE BUYING POKÉ BALLS FROM THE AETHER FOUNDATION, IS THAT RIGHT?!
I HAVE AN IDEA! WHY DON'T YOU DUMP THE AETHER FOUNDATION AND BUY THEM FROM *ME* INSTEAD?
IF YOU HELP US GO BACK TO ALOLA I CAN SELL THEM TO YOU!
AND SINCE FOUR PEOPLE CAN'T RIDE LUNALA AT ONCE, AT LEAST LET MS. CUSTOMER PACKAGE GO AHEAD OF ME.
THAT'S ALL OUT OF THE QUES-TION.
HOW COME?
slam dam mp
SIMPLE...
klttr klttr
BOOM
AIIEE!

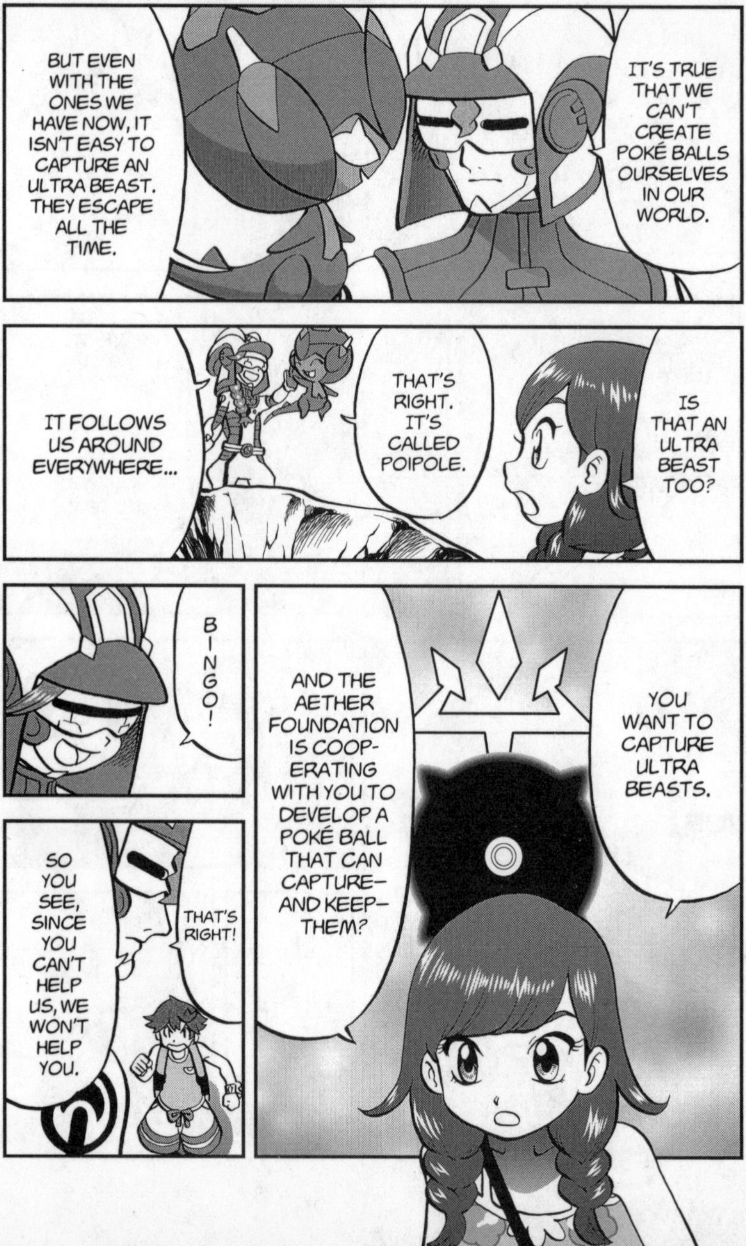
IT'S TRUE THAT WE CAN'T CREATE POKÉ BALLS OURSELVES IN OUR WORLD.
BUT EVEN WITH THE ONES WE HAVE NOW, IT ISN'T EASY TO CAPTURE AN ULTRA BEAST. THEY ESCAPE ALL THE TIME.
IS THAT AN ULTRA BEAST TOO?
THAT'S RIGHT. IT'S CALLED POIPOLE.
IT FOLLOWS US AROUND EVERYWHERE...
YOU WANT TO CAPTURE ULTRA BEASTS.
AND THE AETHER FOUNDATION IS COOP-ERATING WITH YOU TO DEVELOP A POKÉ BALL THAT CAN CAPTURE—AND KEEP—THEM?
BINGO!
THAT'S RIGHT!
SO YOU SEE, SINCE YOU CAN'T HELP US, WE WON'T HELP YOU.

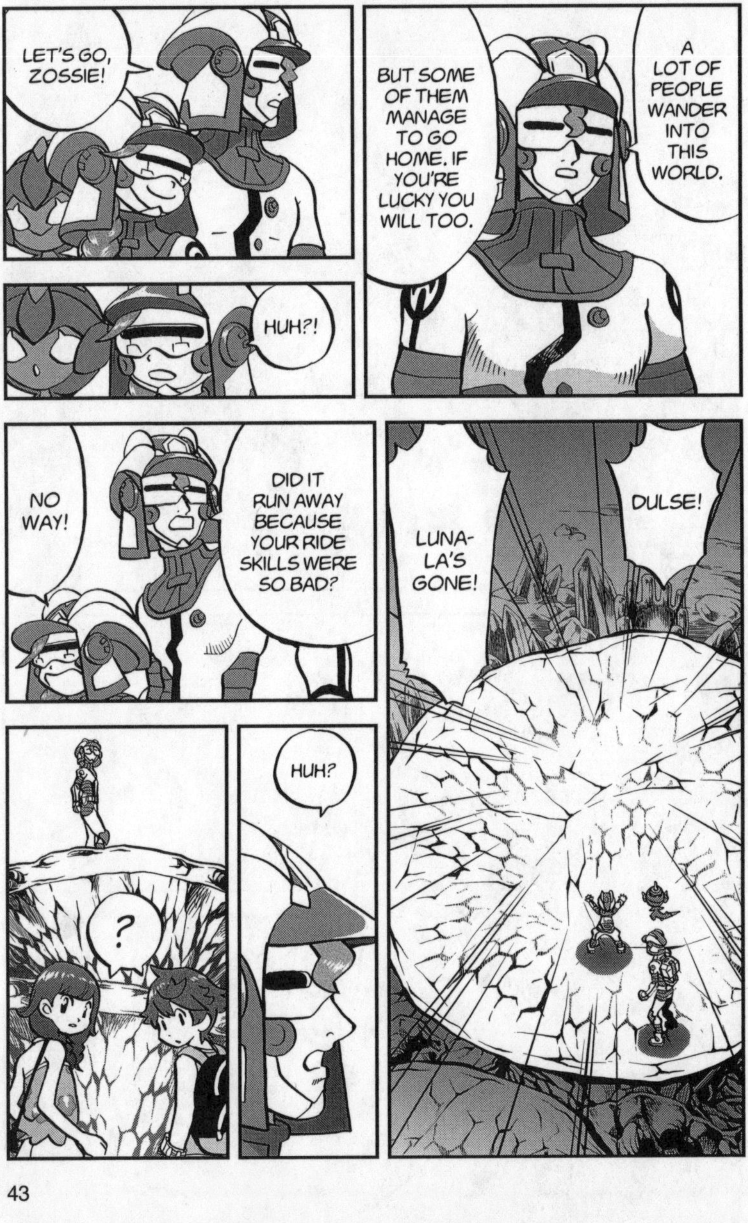
A LOT OF PEOPLE WANDER INTO THIS WORLD.
BUT SOME OF THEM MANAGE TO GO HOME. IF YOU'RE LUCKY YOU WILL TOO.
LET'S GO, ZOSSIE!
HUH?!
DULSE!
LUNA-LA'S GONE!
DID IT RUN AWAY BECAUSE YOUR RIDE SKILLS WERE SO BAD?
NO WAY!
HUH?
?

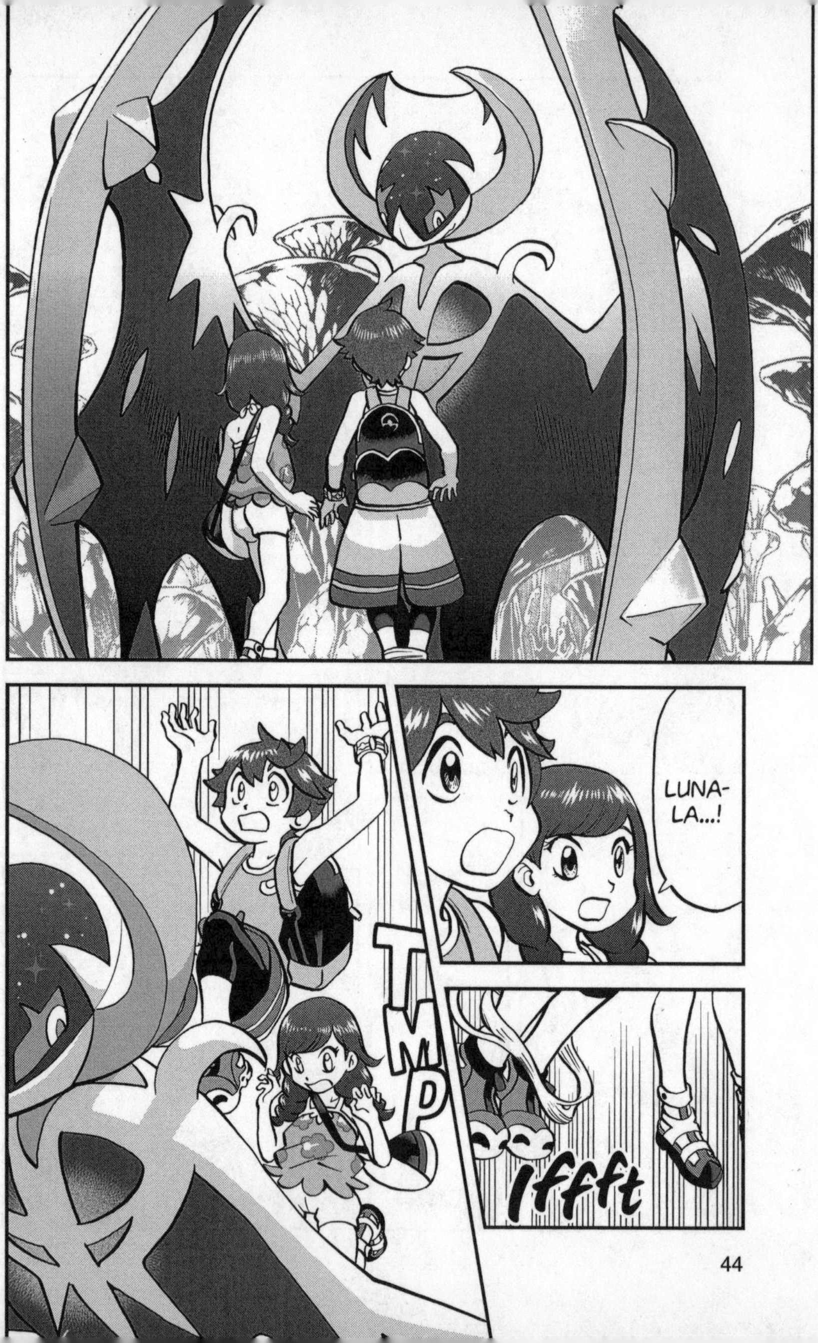
LUNA-
LA...!
ffft
TMP

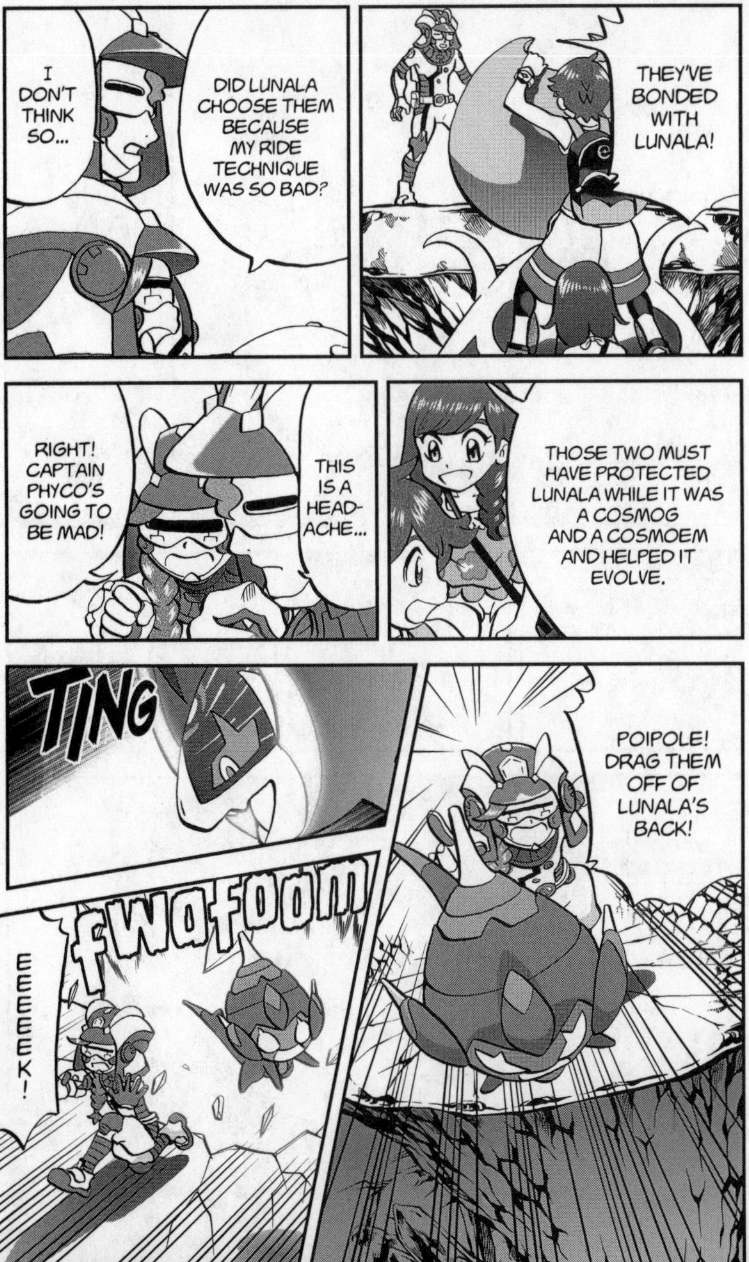
THEY'VE BONDED WITH LUNALA!
DID LUNALA CHOOSE THEM BECAUSE MY RIDE TECHNIQUE WAS SO BAD?
I DON'T THINK SO...
THOSE TWO MUST HAVE PROTECTED LUNALA WHILE IT WAS A COSMOG AND A COSMOEM AND HELPED IT EVOLVE.
THIS IS A HEAD-ACHE...
RIGHT! CAPTAIN PHYCO'S GOING TO BE MAD!
POIPOLE! DRAG THEM OFF OF LUNALA'S BACK!
TING
fwafoom
EEEEEEK!

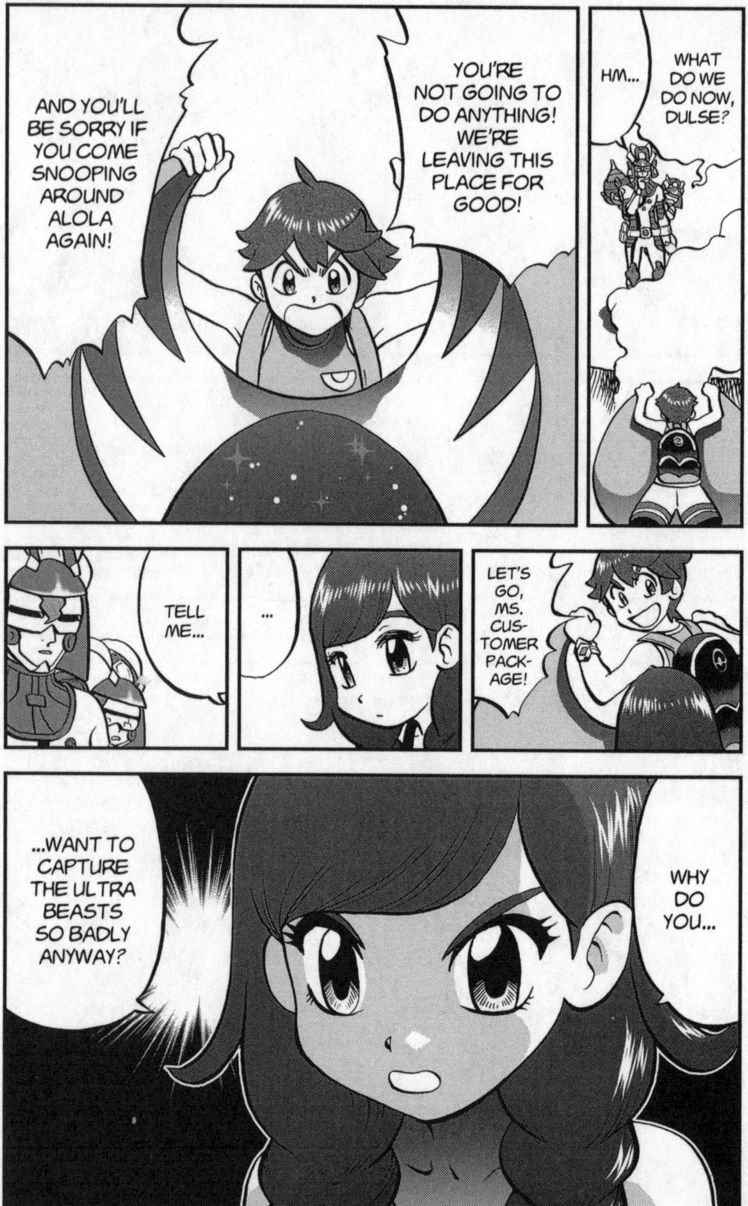
WHAT DO WE DO NOW, DULSE?
HM...
YOU'RE NOT GOING TO DO ANYTHING! WE'RE LEAVING THIS PLACE FOR GOOD!
AND YOU'LL BE SORRY IF YOU COME SNOOPING AROUND ALOLA AGAIN!
LET'S GO, MS. CUS-TOMER PACK-AGE!
...
TELL ME...
WHY DO YOU...
...WANT TO CAPTURE THE ULTRA BEASTS SO BADLY ANYWAY?

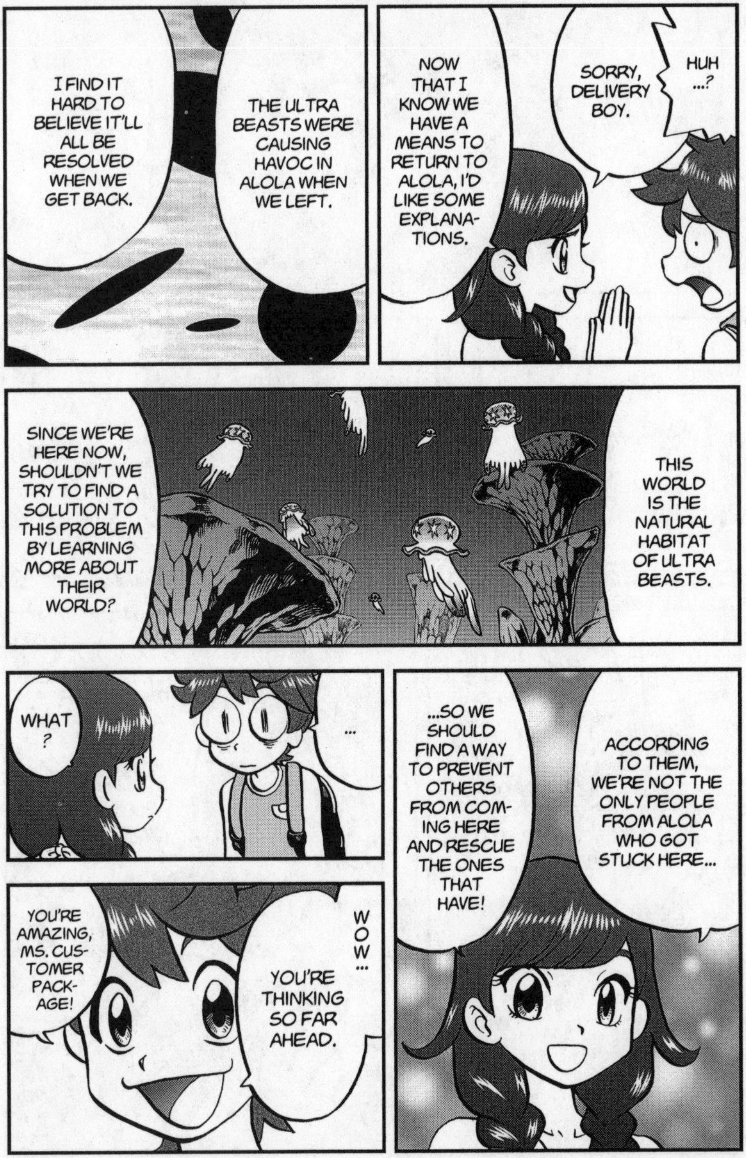
HUH ...?
SORRY, DELIVERY BOY.
NOW THAT I KNOW WE HAVE A MEANS TO RETURN TO ALOLA, I'D LIKE SOME EXPLANA-TIONS.
THE ULTRA BEASTS WERE CAUSING HAVOC IN ALOLA WHEN WE LEFT.
I FIND IT HARD TO BELIEVE IT'LL ALL BE RESOLVED WHEN WE GET BACK.
THIS WORLD IS THE NATURAL HABITAT OF ULTRA BEASTS.
SINCE WE'RE HERE NOW, SHOULDN'T WE TRY TO FIND A SOLUTION TO THIS PROBLEM BY LEARNING MORE ABOUT THEIR WORLD?
ACCORDING TO THEM, WE'RE NOT THE ONLY PEOPLE FROM ALOLA WHO GOT STUCK HERE...
...SO WE SHOULD FIND A WAY TO PREVENT OTHERS FROM COM-ING HERE AND RESCUE THE ONES THAT HAVE!
...
WHAT ?
WOW...
YOU'RE THINKING SO FAR AHEAD.
YOU'RE AMAZING, MS. CUS-TOMER PACK-AGE!

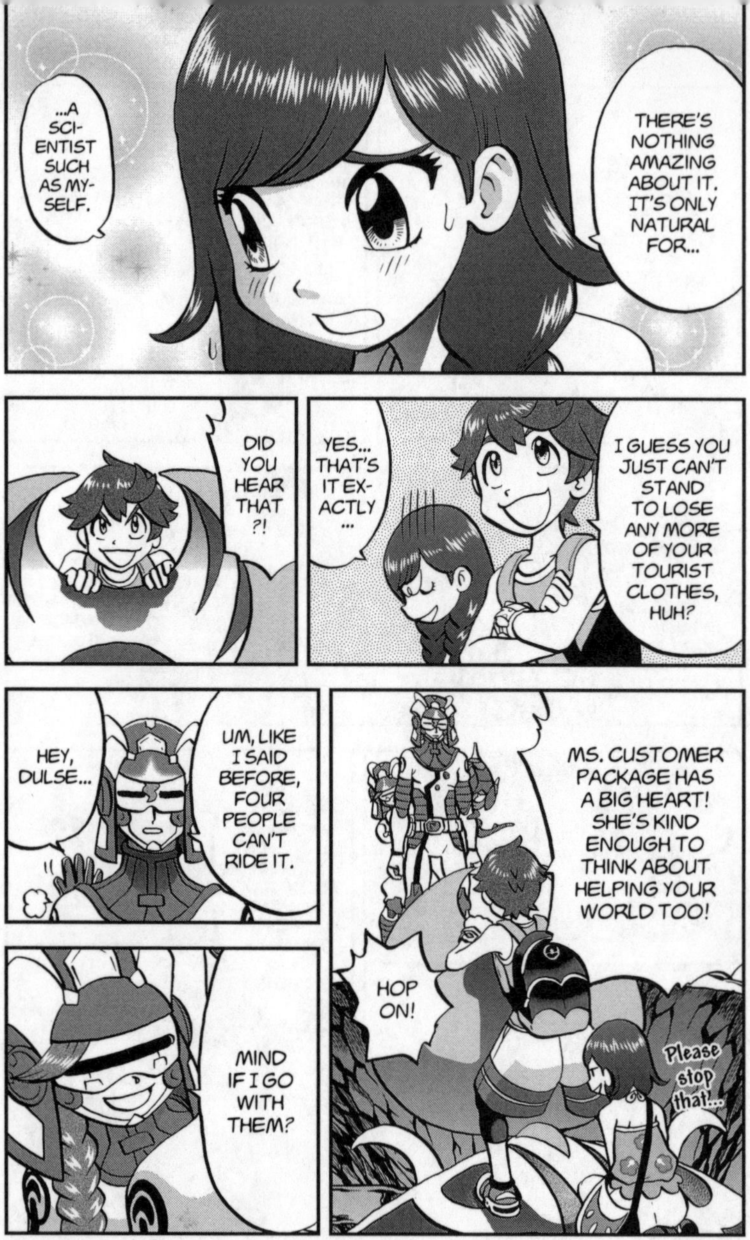
THERE'S NOTHING AMAZING ABOUT IT. IT'S ONLY NATURAL FOR...
...A SCI-ENTIST SUCH AS MY-SELF.
I GUESS YOU JUST CAN'T STAND TO LOSE ANY MORE OF YOUR TOURIST CLOTHES, HUH?
YES... THAT'S IT EX-ACTLY ...
DID YOU HEAR THAT ?!
MS. CUSTOMER PACKAGE HAS A BIG HEART! SHE'S KIND ENOUGH TO THINK ABOUT HELPING YOUR WORLD TOO!
HOP ON!
Please stop that...
UM, LIKE I SAID BEFORE, FOUR PEOPLE CAN'T RIDE IT.
HEY, DULSE...
MIND IF I GO WITH THEM?

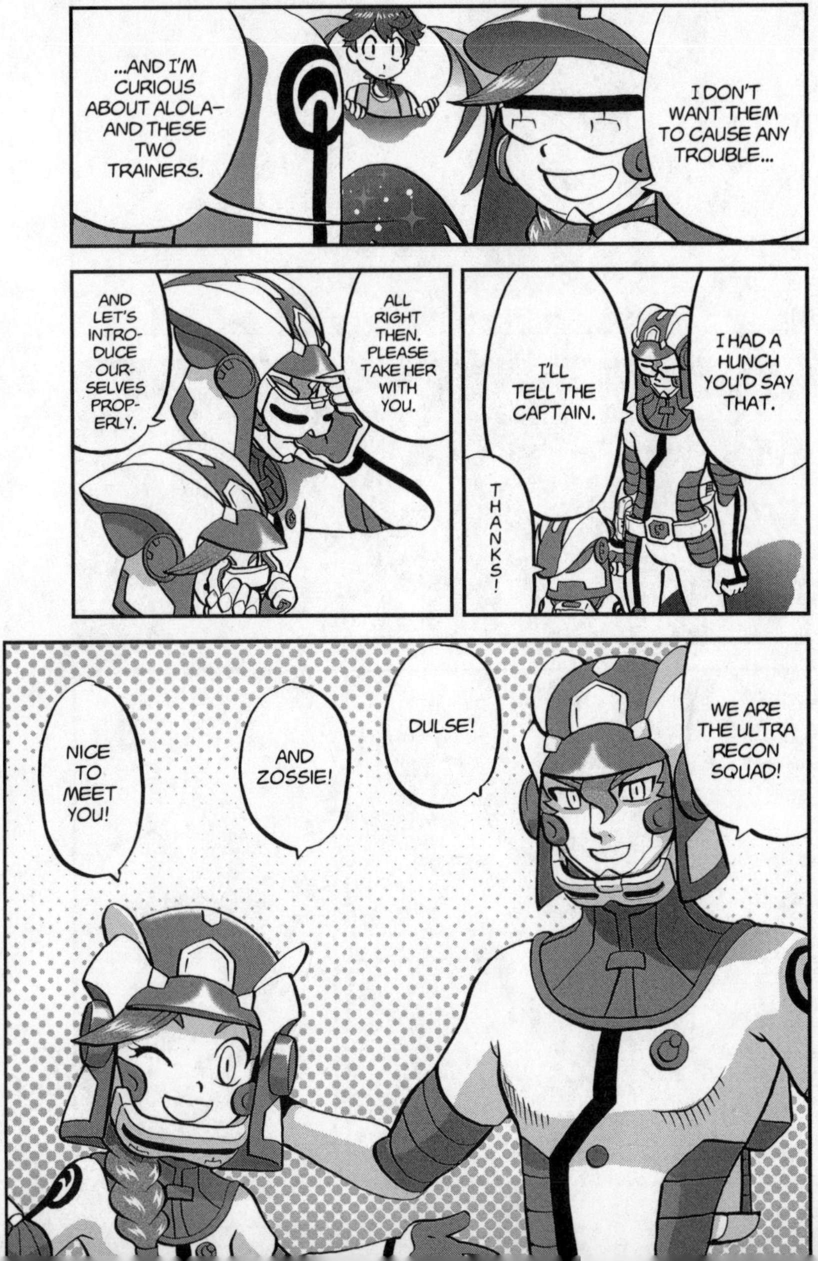
I DON'T WANT THEM TO CAUSE ANY TROUBLE...
...AND I'M CURIOUS ABOUT ALOLA— AND THESE TWO TRAINERS.
I HAD A HUNCH YOU'D SAY THAT.
I'LL TELL THE CAPTAIN.
THANKS!
ALL RIGHT THEN. PLEASE TAKE HER WITH YOU.
AND LET'S INTRODUCE OURSELVES PROPERLY.
WE ARE THE ULTRA RECON SQUAD!
DULSE!
AND ZOSSIE!
NICE TO MEET YOU!

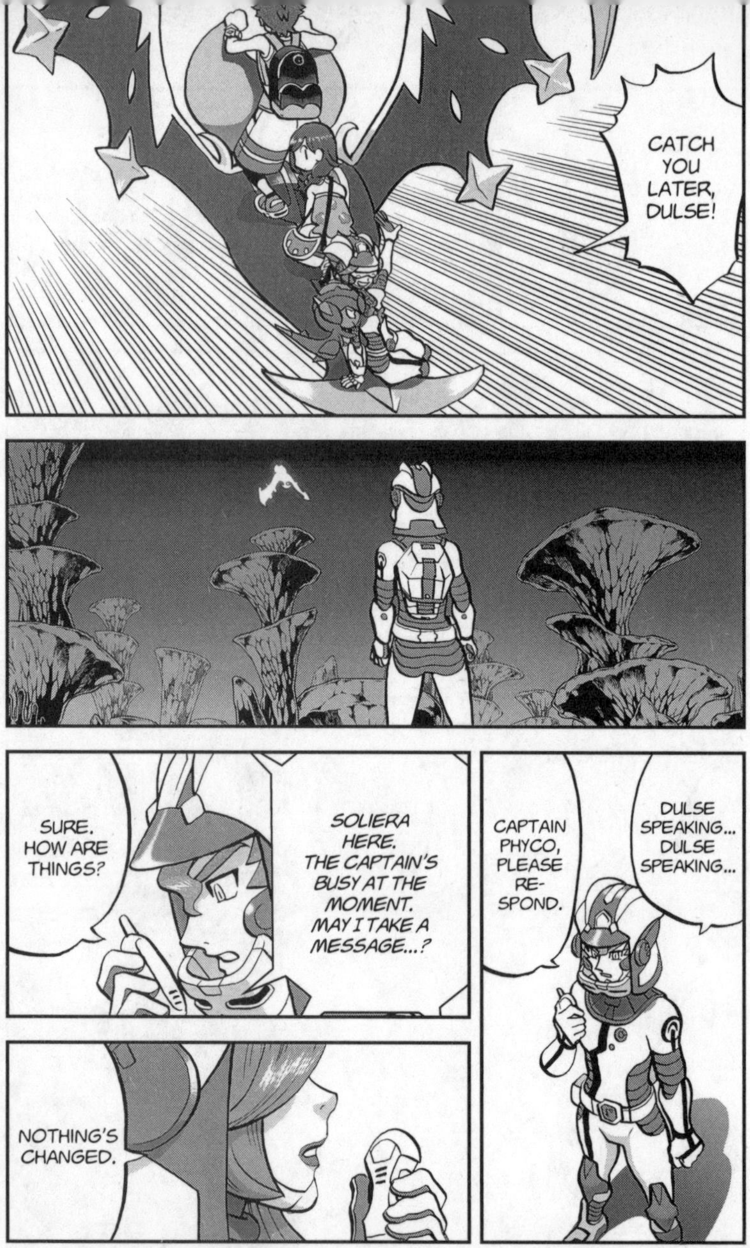
CATCH YOU LATER, DULSE!
DULSE SPEAKING... DULSE SPEAKING...
CAPTAIN PHYCO, PLEASE RE-SPOND.
SOLIERA HERE. THE CAPTAIN'S BUSY AT THE MOMENT. MAY I TAKE A MESSAGE...?
SURE. HOW ARE THINGS?
NOTHING'S CHANGED.

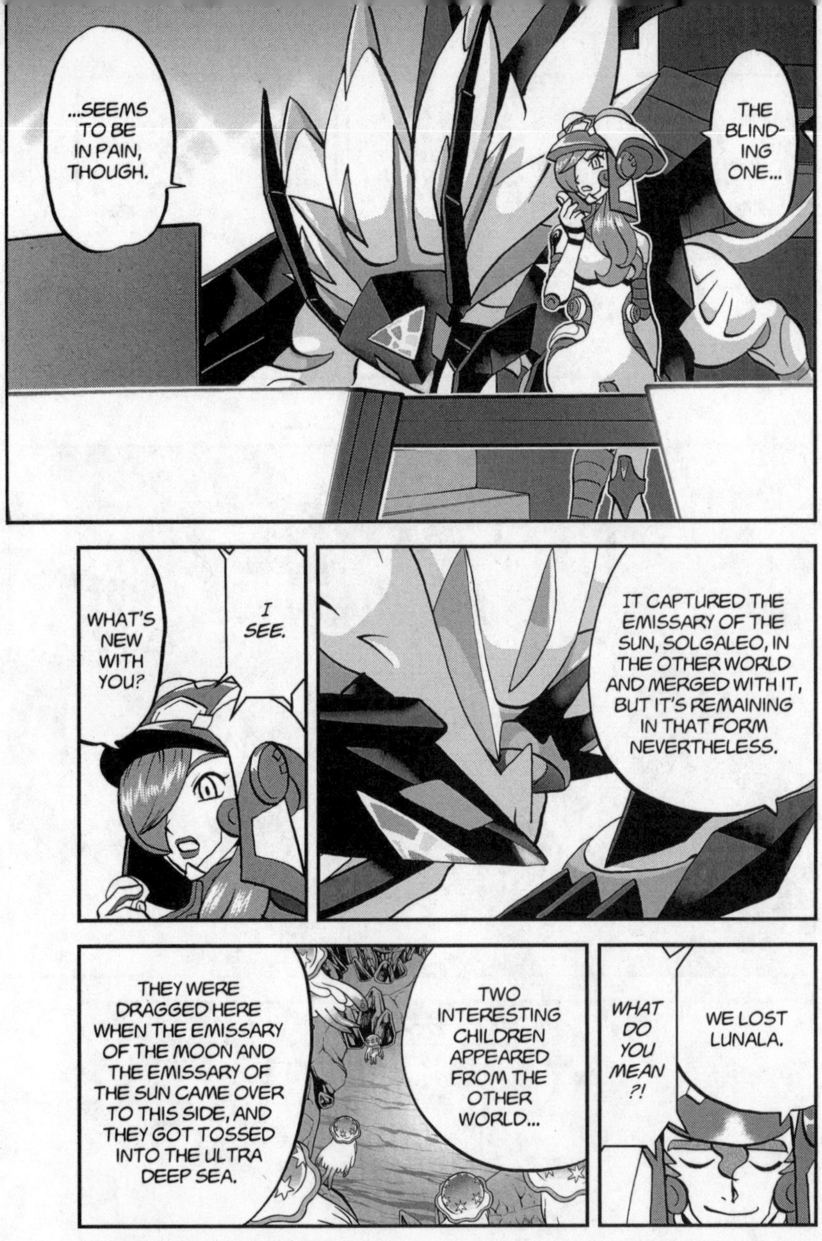
THE BLINDING ONE...
...SEEMS TO BE IN PAIN, THOUGH.
IT CAPTURED THE EMISSARY OF THE SUN, SOLGALEO, IN THE OTHER WORLD AND MERGED WITH IT, BUT IT'S REMAINING IN THAT FORM NEVERTHELESS.
I SEE.
WHAT'S NEW WITH YOU?
WE LOST LUNALA.
WHAT DO YOU MEAN?!
TWO INTERESTING CHILDREN APPEARED FROM THE OTHER WORLD...
THEY WERE DRAGGED HERE WHEN THE EMISSARY OF THE MOON AND THE EMISSARY OF THE SUN CAME OVER TO THIS SIDE, AND THEY GOT TOSSED INTO THE ULTRA DEEP SEA.

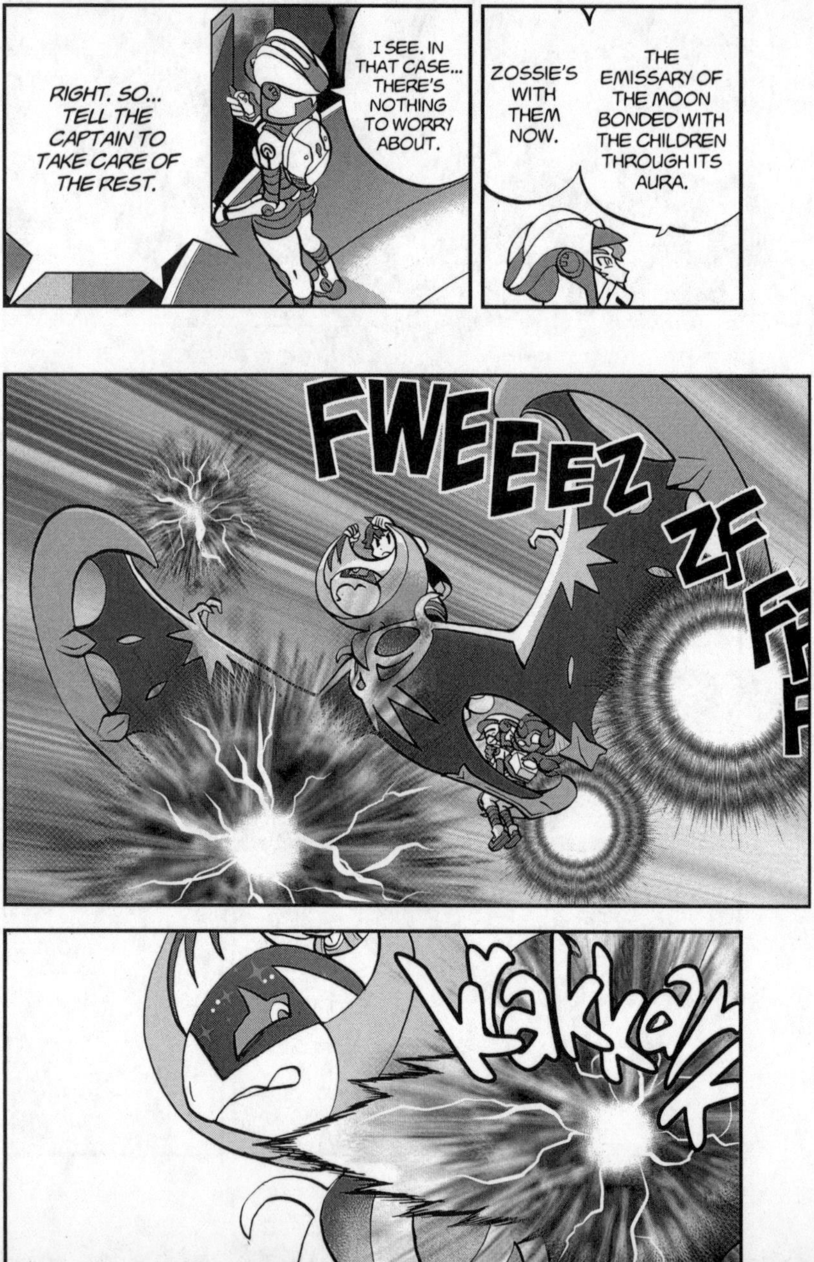
THE EMISSARY OF THE MOON BONDED WITH THE CHILDREN THROUGH ITS AURA.
ZOSSIE'S WITH THEM NOW.
I SEE. IN THAT CASE... THERE'S NOTHING TO WORRY ABOUT.
RIGHT. SO... TELL THE CAPTAIN TO TAKE CARE OF THE REST.
FWEEEZ
ZFFFF
VRAKKAK

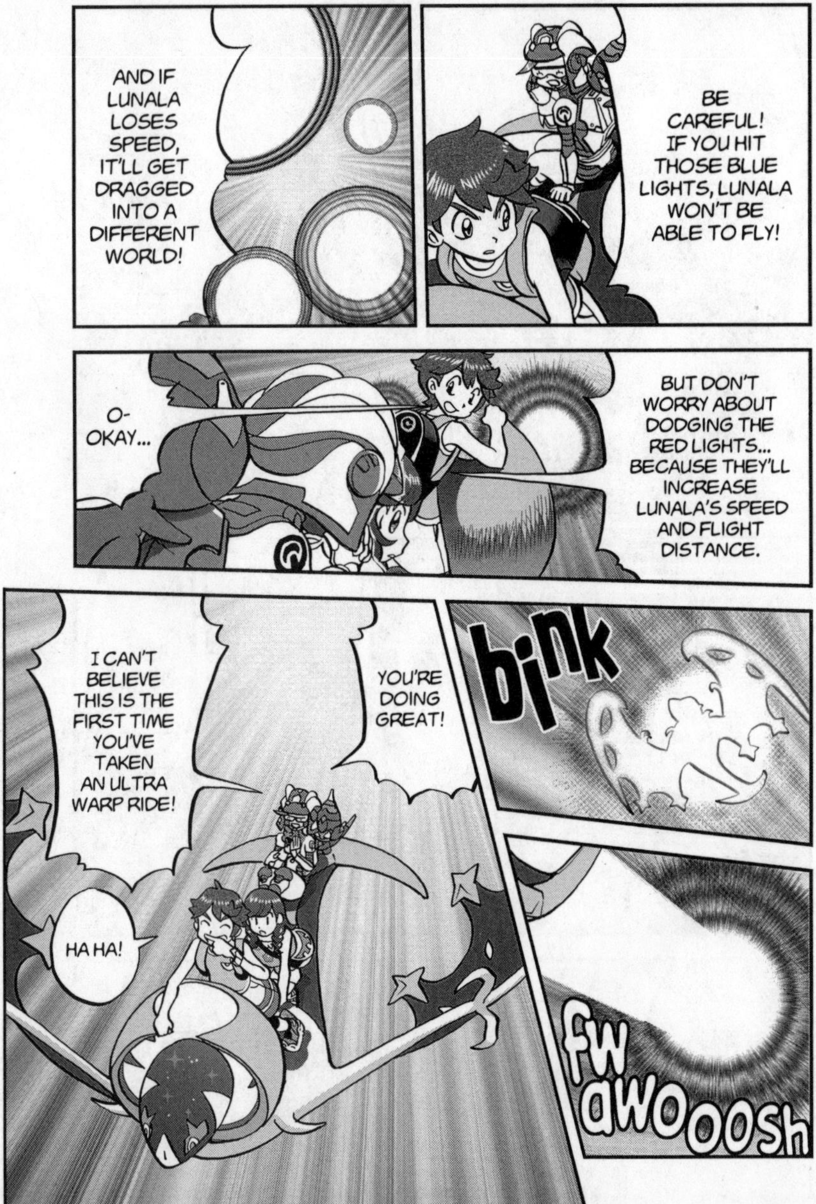
BE CAREFUL! IF YOU HIT THOSE BLUE LIGHTS, LUNALA WON'T BE ABLE TO FLY!
AND IF LUNALA LOSES SPEED, IT'LL GET DRAGGED INTO A DIFFERENT WORLD!
BUT DON'T WORRY ABOUT DODGING THE RED LIGHTS... BECAUSE THEY'LL INCREASE LUNALA'S SPEED AND FLIGHT DISTANCE.
O- OKAY...
bink
fw awooosh
YOU'RE DOING GREAT!
I CAN'T BELIEVE THIS IS THE FIRST TIME YOU'VE TAKEN AN ULTRA WARP RIDE!
HA HA!

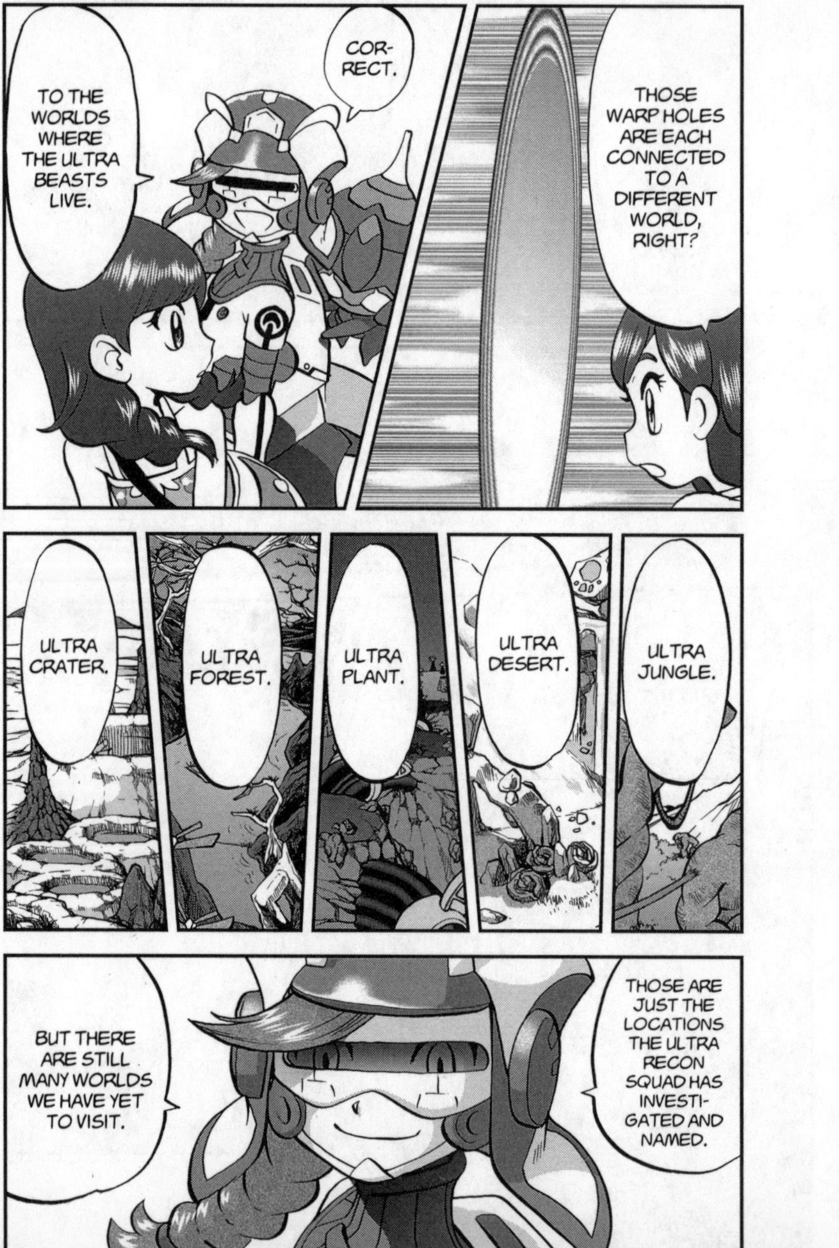
THOSE WARP HOLES ARE EACH CONNECTED TO A DIFFERENT WORLD, RIGHT?
COR-RECT.
TO THE WORLDS WHERE THE ULTRA BEASTS LIVE.
ULTRA JUNGLE.
ULTRA DESERT.
ULTRA PLANT.
ULTRA FOREST.
ULTRA CRATER.
THOSE ARE JUST THE LOCATIONS THE ULTRA RECON SQUAD HAS INVESTI-GATED AND NAMED.
BUT THERE ARE STILL MANY WORLDS WE HAVE YET TO VISIT.

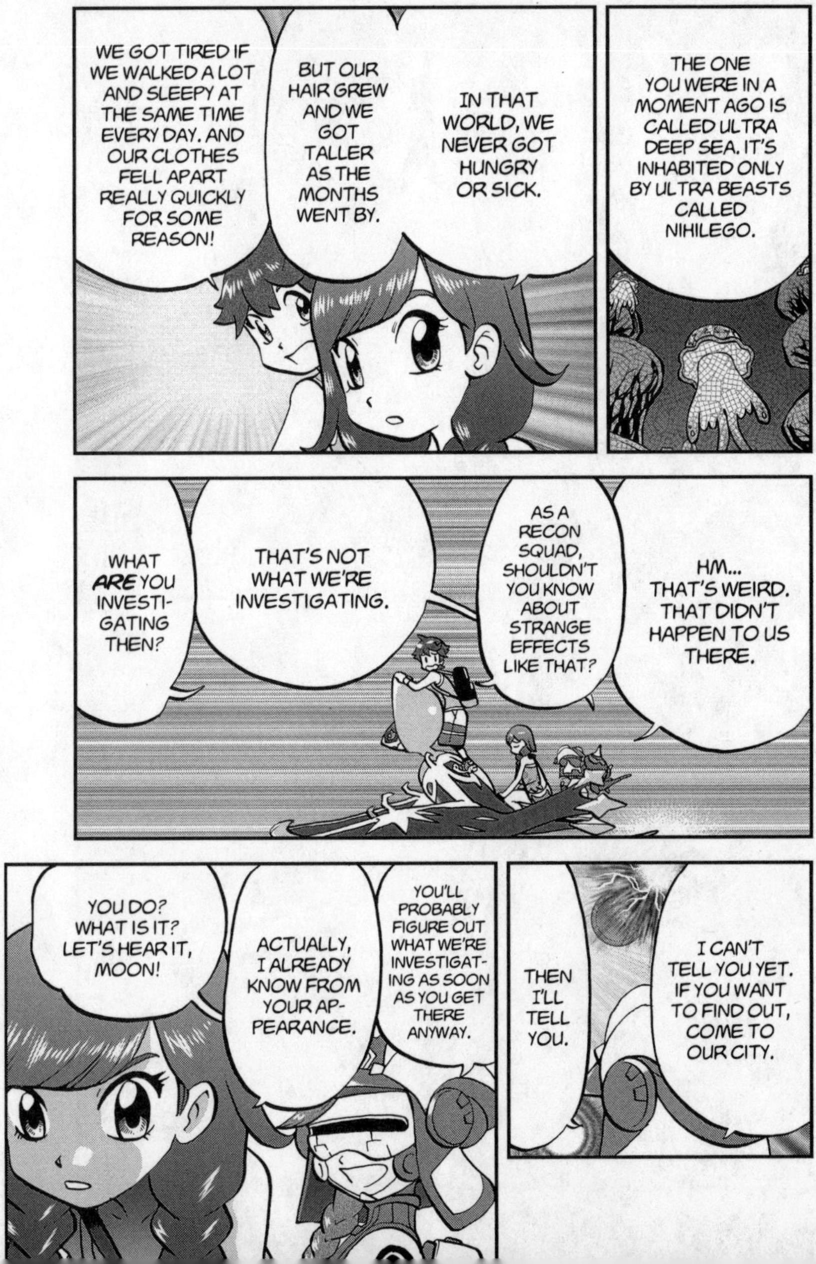
THE ONE YOU WERE IN A MOMENT AGO IS CALLED ULTRA DEEP SEA. IT'S INHABITED ONLY BY ULTRA BEASTS CALLED NIHILEGO.
IN THAT WORLD, WE NEVER GOT HUNGRY OR SICK.
BUT OUR HAIR GREW AND WE GOT TALLER AS THE MONTHS WENT BY.
WE GOT TIRED IF WE WALKED A LOT AND SLEEPY AT THE SAME TIME EVERY DAY. AND OUR CLOTHES FELL APART REALLY QUICKLY FOR SOME REASON!
HM... THAT'S WEIRD. THAT DIDN'T HAPPEN TO US THERE.
AS A RECON SQUAD, SHOULDN'T YOU KNOW ABOUT STRANGE EFFECTS LIKE THAT?
THAT'S NOT WHAT WE'RE INVESTIGATING.
WHAT *ARE* YOU INVESTI-GATING THEN?
I CAN'T TELL YOU YET. IF YOU WANT TO FIND OUT, COME TO OUR CITY.
THEN I'LL TELL YOU.
YOU'LL PROBABLY FIGURE OUT WHAT WE'RE INVESTIGAT-ING AS SOON AS YOU GET THERE ANYWAY.
ACTUALLY, I ALREADY KNOW FROM YOUR AP-PEARANCE.
YOU DO? WHAT IS IT? LET'S HEAR IT, MOON!

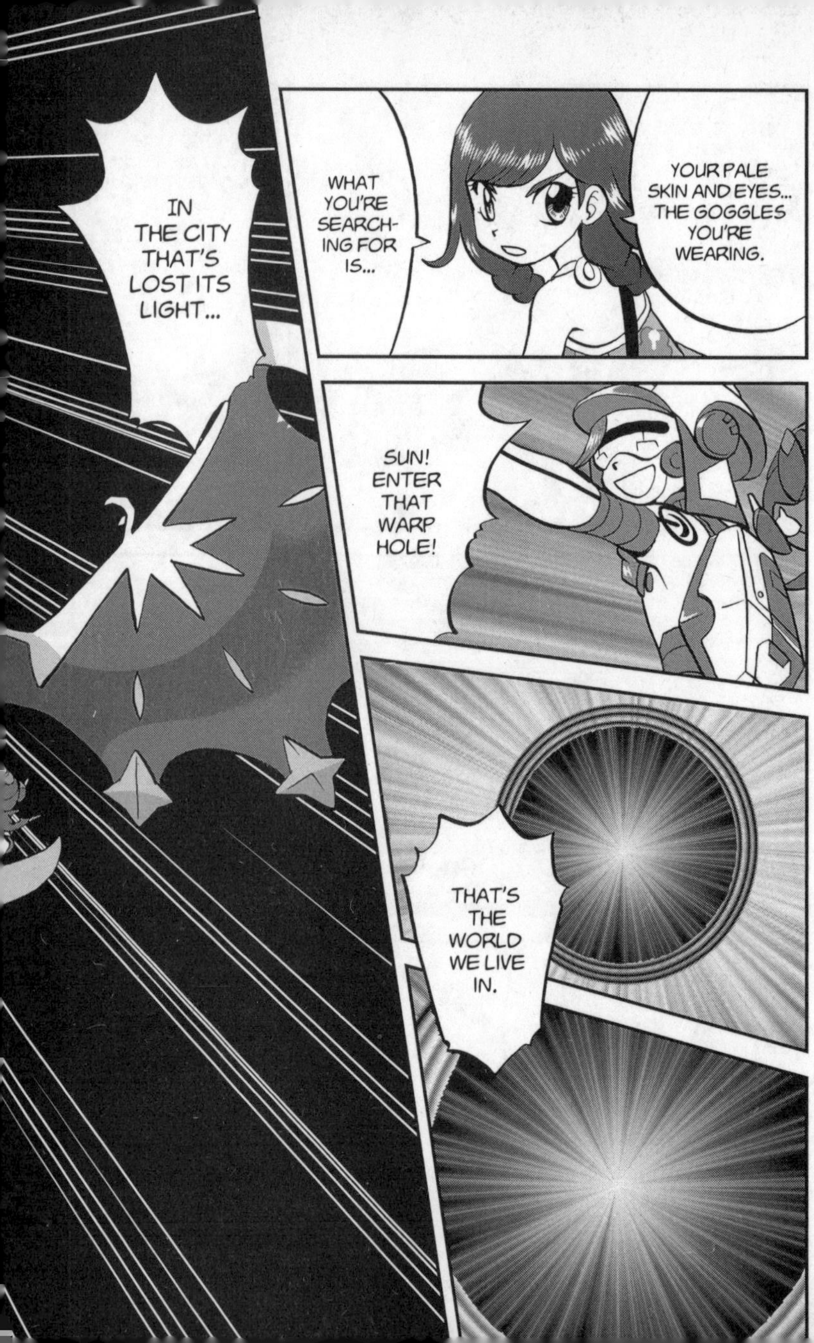
YOUR PALE SKIN AND EYES... THE GOGGLES YOU'RE WEARING.
WHAT YOU'RE SEARCH-ING FOR IS...
SUN! ENTER THAT WARP HOLE!
THAT'S THE WORLD WE LIVE IN.
IN THE CITY THAT'S LOST ITS LIGHT...

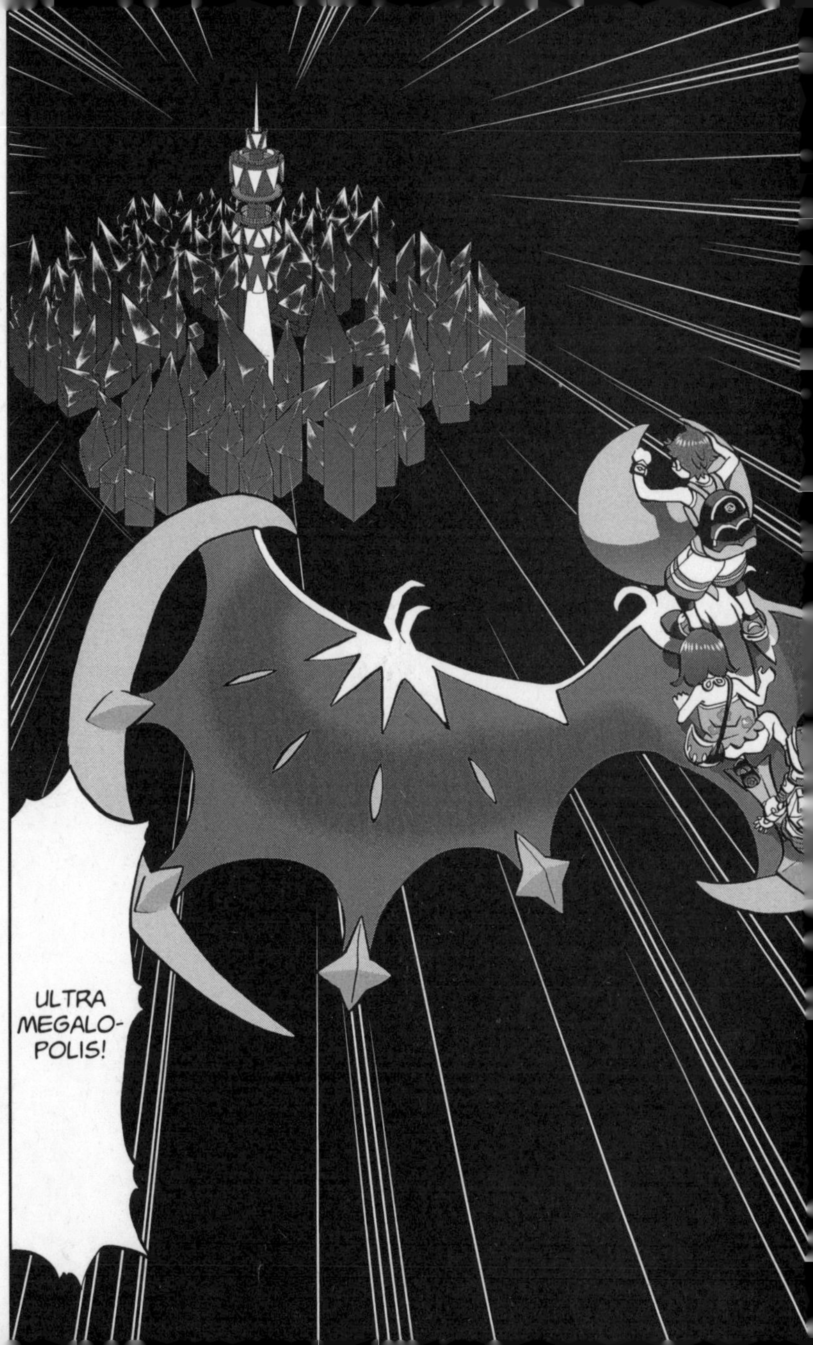
ULTRA MEGALO-POLIS!

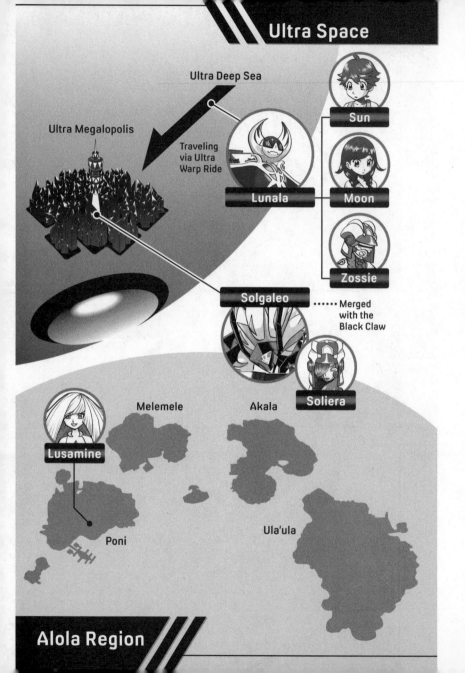

Ultra Space

Ultra Deep Sea

Ultra Megalopolis

Traveling via Ultra Warp Ride

Sun

Lunala

Moon

Zossie

Solgaleo ····· Merged with the Black Claw

Soliera

Melemele

Akala

Lusamine

Poni

Ula'ula

Alola Region

Adventure 28
Arrival at the Scientific Megalopolis

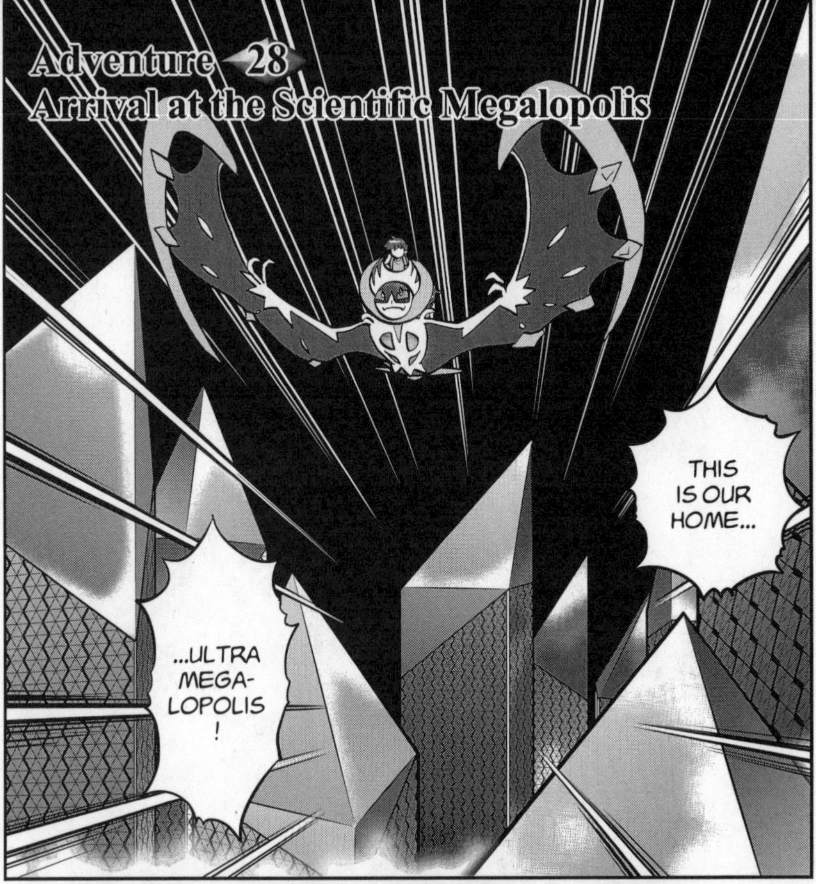
THIS IS OUR HOME...
...ULTRA MEGA-LOPOLIS!

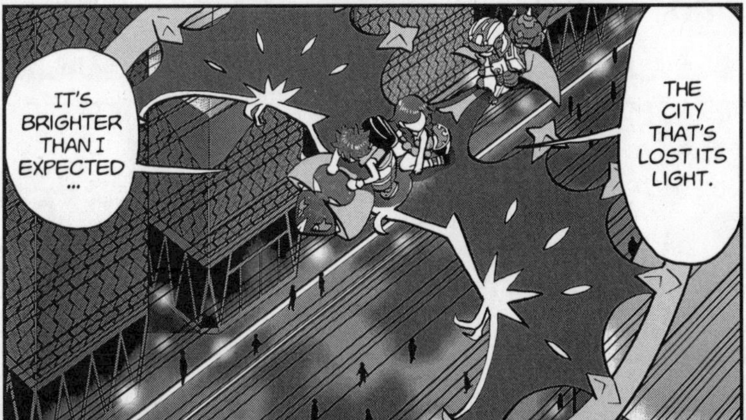
THE CITY THAT'S LOST ITS LIGHT.
IT'S BRIGHTER THAN I EXPECTED...

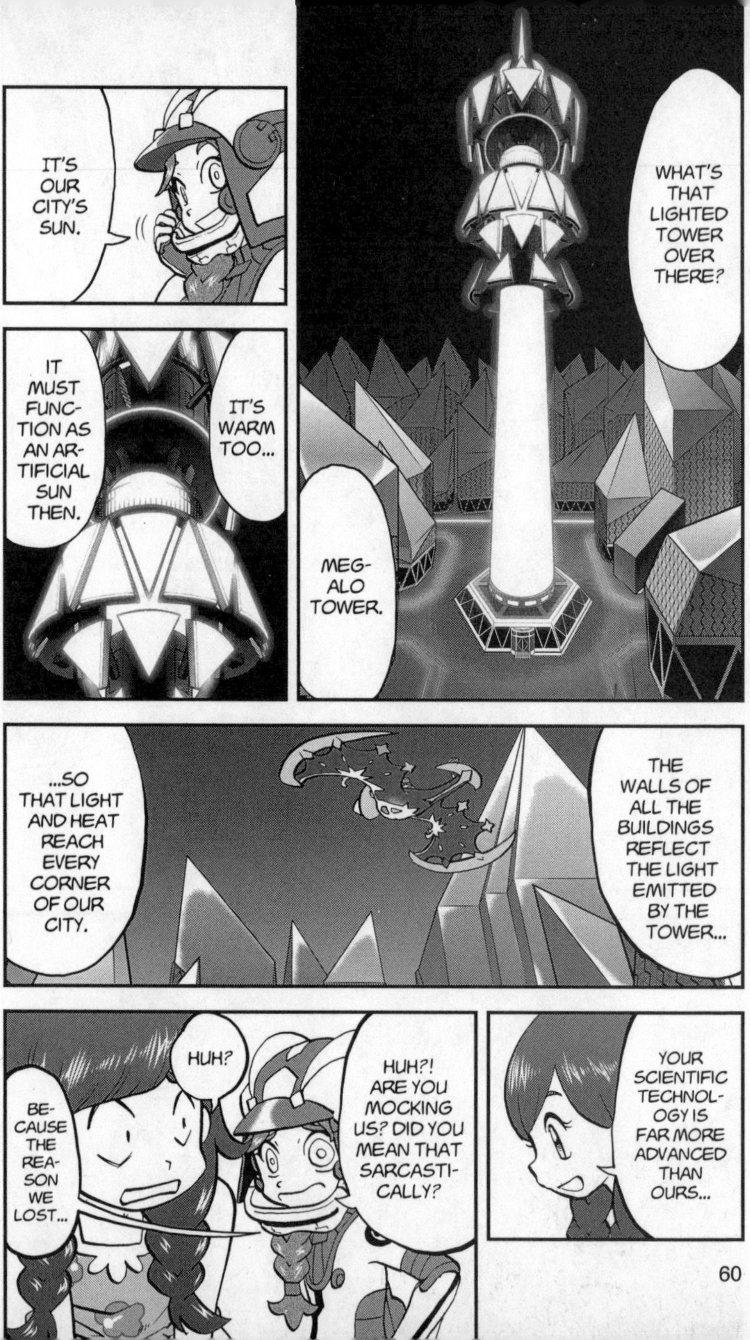
WHAT'S THAT LIGHTED TOWER OVER THERE?
MEG-ALO TOWER.
IT'S OUR CITY'S SUN.
IT'S WARM TOO...
IT MUST FUNC-TION AS AN AR-TIFICIAL SUN THEN.
THE WALLS OF ALL THE BUILDINGS REFLECT THE LIGHT EMITTED BY THE TOWER...
...SO THAT LIGHT AND HEAT REACH EVERY CORNER OF OUR CITY.
YOUR SCIENTIFIC TECHNOL-OGY IS FAR MORE ADVANCED THAN OURS...
HUH?! ARE YOU MOCKING US? DID YOU MEAN THAT SARCASTI-CALLY?
HUH?
BE-CAUSE THE REA-SON WE LOST...

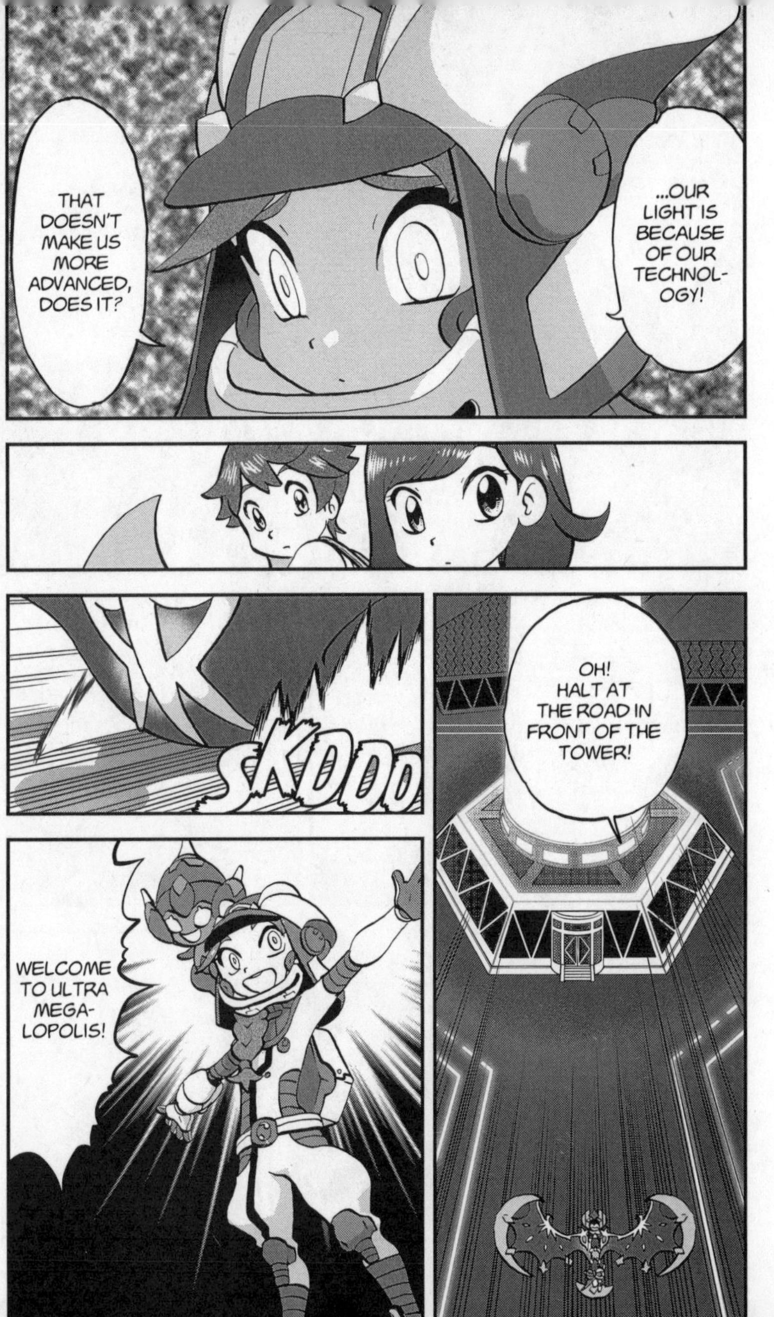
...OUR LIGHT IS BECAUSE OF OUR TECHNOLOGY!
THAT DOESN'T MAKE US MORE ADVANCED, DOES IT?
OH! HALT AT THE ROAD IN FRONT OF THE TOWER!
SKDOOO
WELCOME TO ULTRA MEGALOPOLIS!

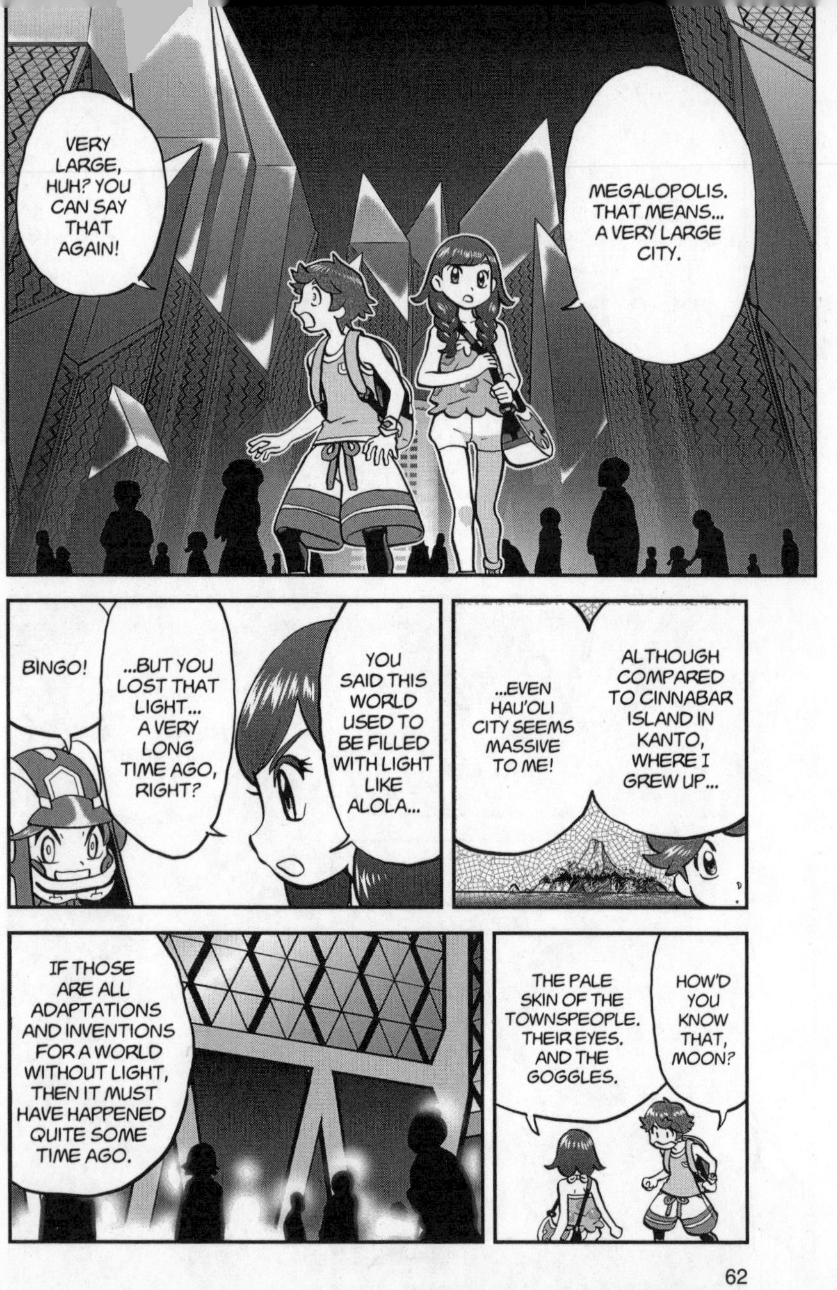
MEGALOPOLIS. THAT MEANS... A VERY LARGE CITY.
VERY LARGE, HUH? YOU CAN SAY THAT AGAIN!
ALTHOUGH COMPARED TO CINNABAR ISLAND IN KANTO, WHERE I GREW UP...
...EVEN HAU'OLI CITY SEEMS MASSIVE TO ME!
YOU SAID THIS WORLD USED TO BE FILLED WITH LIGHT LIKE ALOLA...
...BUT YOU LOST THAT LIGHT... A VERY LONG TIME AGO, RIGHT?
BINGO!
HOW'D YOU KNOW THAT, MOON?
THE PALE SKIN OF THE TOWNSPEOPLE. THEIR EYES. AND THE GOGGLES.
IF THOSE ARE ALL ADAPTATIONS AND INVENTIONS FOR A WORLD WITHOUT LIGHT, THEN IT MUST HAVE HAPPENED QUITE SOME TIME AGO.

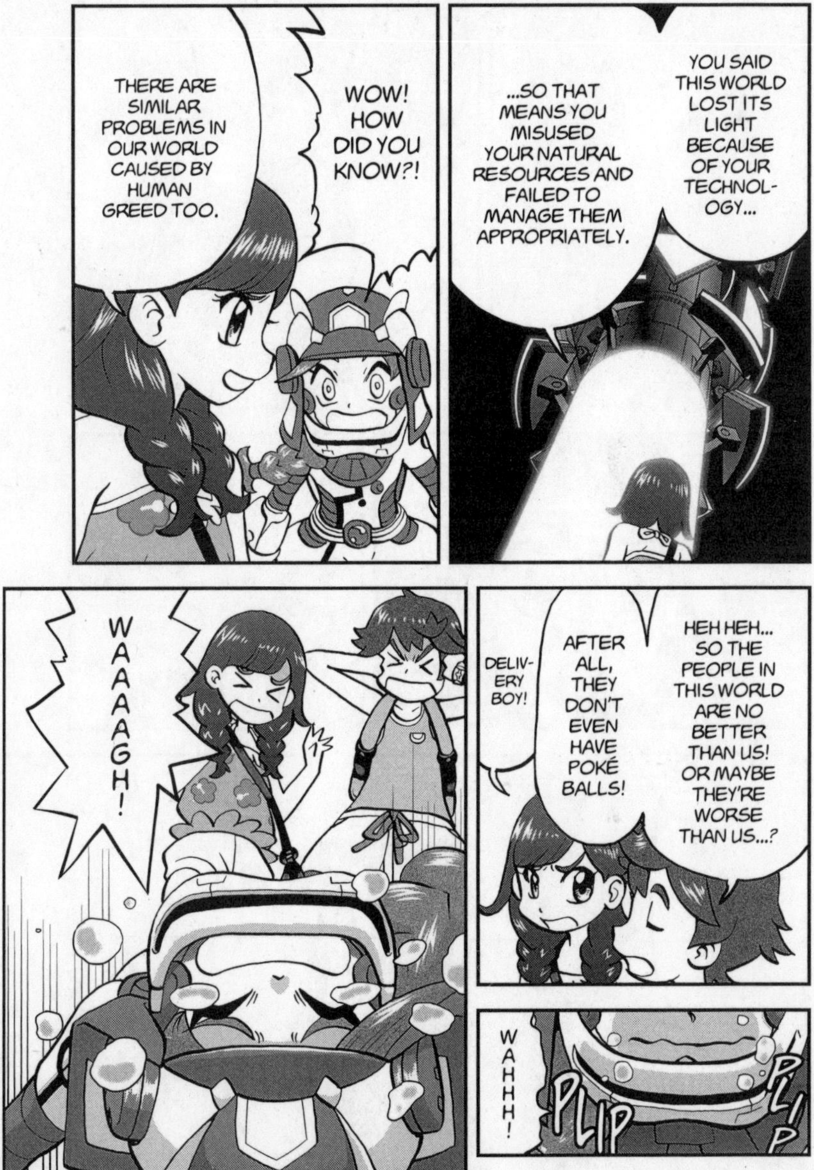
YOU SAID THIS WORLD LOST ITS LIGHT BECAUSE OF YOUR TECHNOLOGY...
...SO THAT MEANS YOU MISUSED YOUR NATURAL RESOURCES AND FAILED TO MANAGE THEM APPROPRIATELY.
WOW! HOW DID YOU KNOW?!
THERE ARE SIMILAR PROBLEMS IN OUR WORLD CAUSED BY HUMAN GREED TOO.
HEH HEH... SO THE PEOPLE IN THIS WORLD ARE NO BETTER THAN US! OR MAYBE THEY'RE WORSE THAN US...?
AFTER ALL, THEY DON'T EVEN HAVE POKÉ BALLS!
DELIVERY BOY!
WAHHH!
PLIP
PLIP
WAAAAAGH!

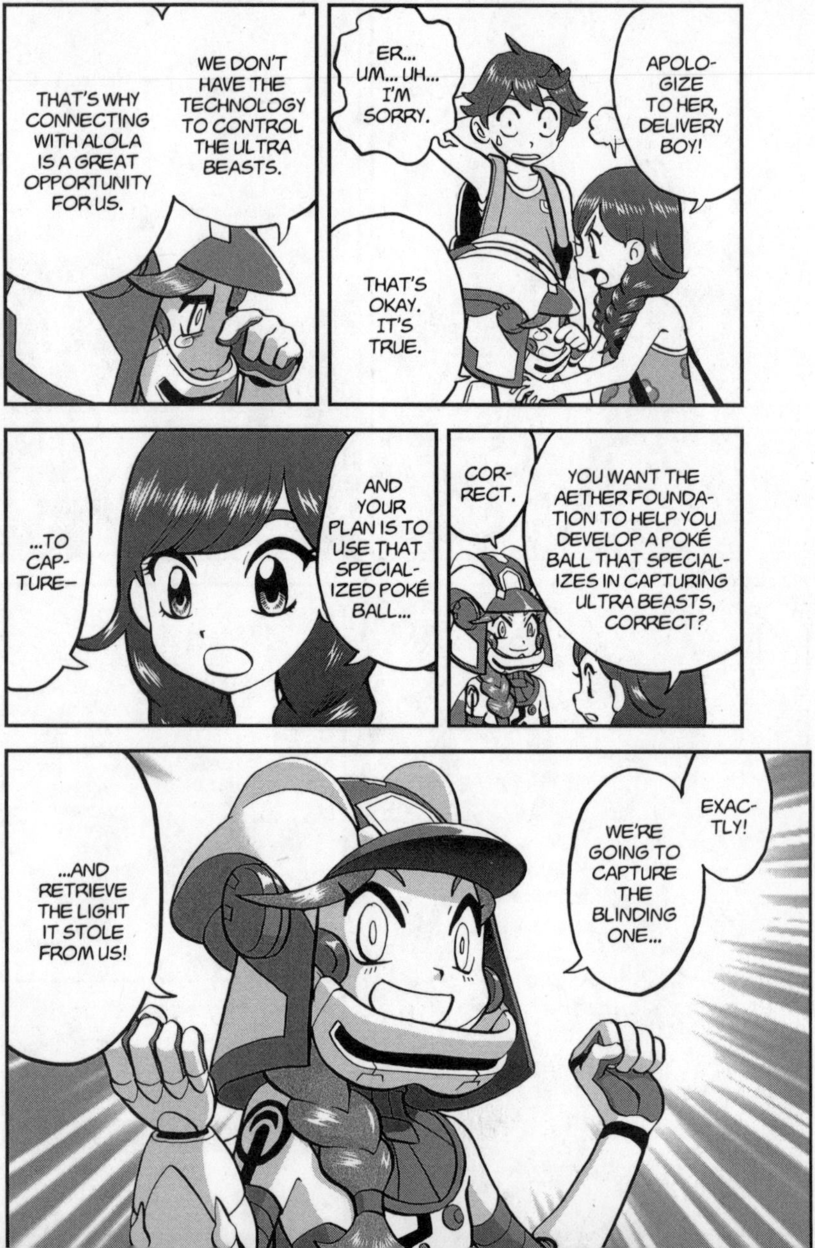
APOLOGIZE TO HER, DELIVERY BOY!
ER... UM... UH... I'M SORRY.
THAT'S OKAY. IT'S TRUE.
WE DON'T HAVE THE TECHNOLOGY TO CONTROL THE ULTRA BEASTS.
THAT'S WHY CONNECTING WITH ALOLA IS A GREAT OPPORTUNITY FOR US.
YOU WANT THE AETHER FOUNDATION TO HELP YOU DEVELOP A POKÉ BALL THAT SPECIALIZES IN CAPTURING ULTRA BEASTS, CORRECT?
CORRECT.
AND YOUR PLAN IS TO USE THAT SPECIALIZED POKÉ BALL...
...TO CAPTURE—
EXACTLY!
WE'RE GOING TO CAPTURE THE BLINDING ONE...
...AND RETRIEVE THE LIGHT IT STOLE FROM US!

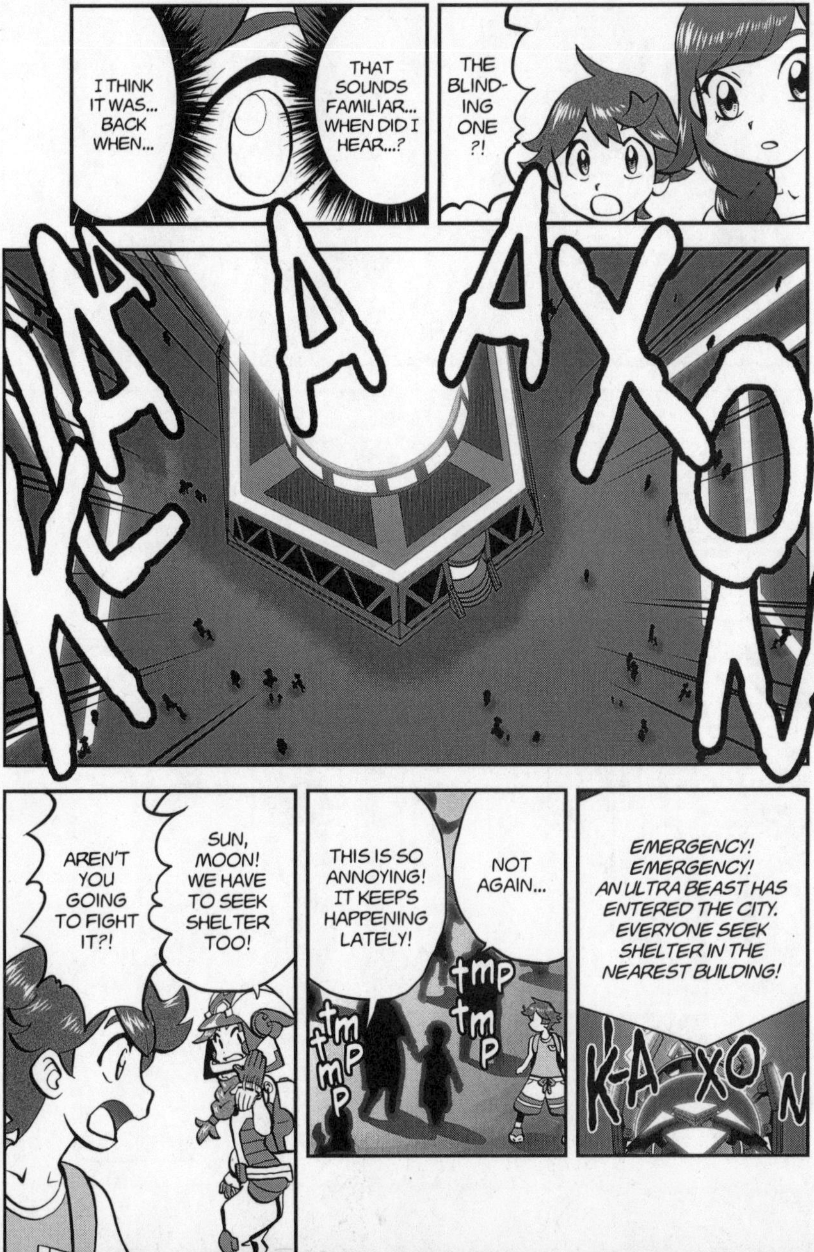
THE BLINDING ONE ?!
THAT SOUNDS FAMILIAR... WHEN DID I HEAR...?
I THINK IT WAS... BACK WHEN...
KAAAXON
EMERGENCY! EMERGENCY! AN ULTRA BEAST HAS ENTERED THE CITY. EVERYONE SEEK SHELTER IN THE NEAREST BUILDING!
K-A-XON
NOT AGAIN...
THIS IS SO ANNOYING! IT KEEPS HAPPENING LATELY!
tmp tmp
tmp tmp
SUN, MOON! WE HAVE TO SEEK SHELTER TOO!
AREN'T YOU GOING TO FIGHT IT?!

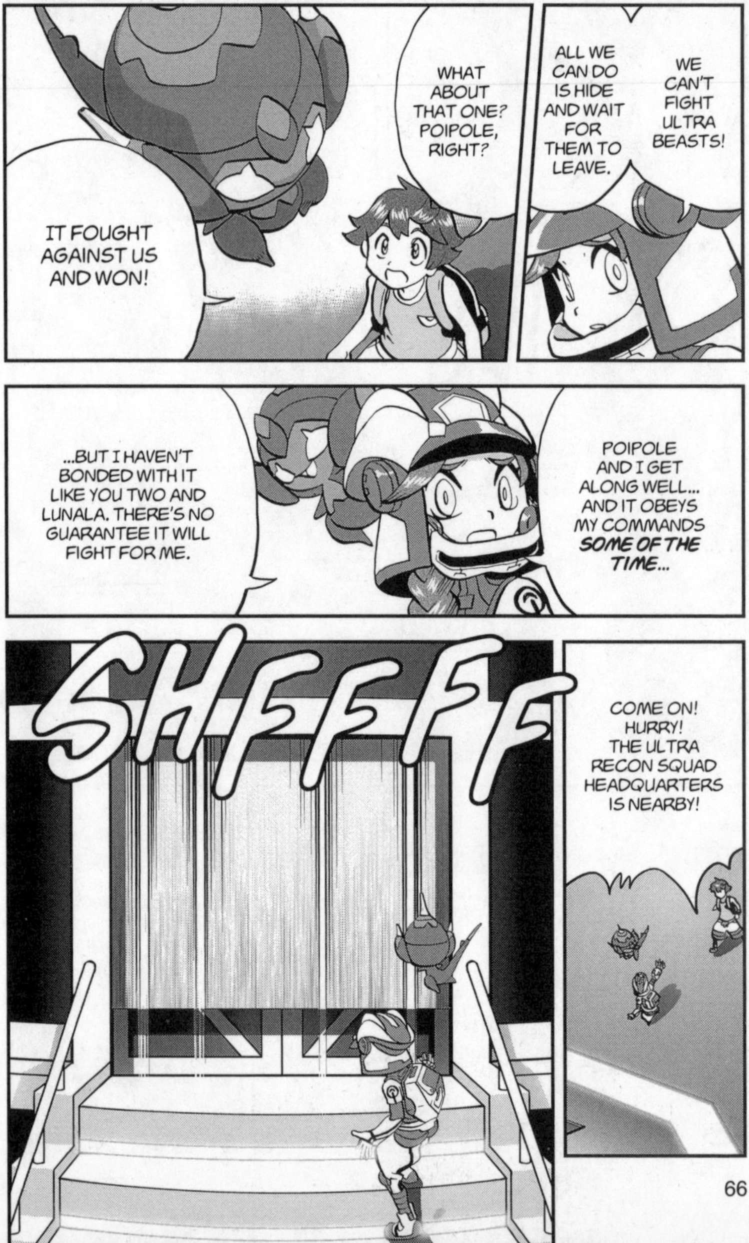
WE CAN'T FIGHT ULTRA BEASTS!
ALL WE CAN DO IS HIDE AND WAIT FOR THEM TO LEAVE.
WHAT ABOUT THAT ONE? POIPOLE, RIGHT?
IT FOUGHT AGAINST US AND WON!
POIPOLE AND I GET ALONG WELL... AND IT OBEYS MY COMMANDS *SOME OF THE TIME...*
...BUT I HAVEN'T BONDED WITH IT LIKE YOU TWO AND LUNALA. THERE'S NO GUARANTEE IT WILL FIGHT FOR ME.
COME ON! HURRY! THE ULTRA RECON SQUAD HEADQUARTERS IS NEARBY!
SHFFFF

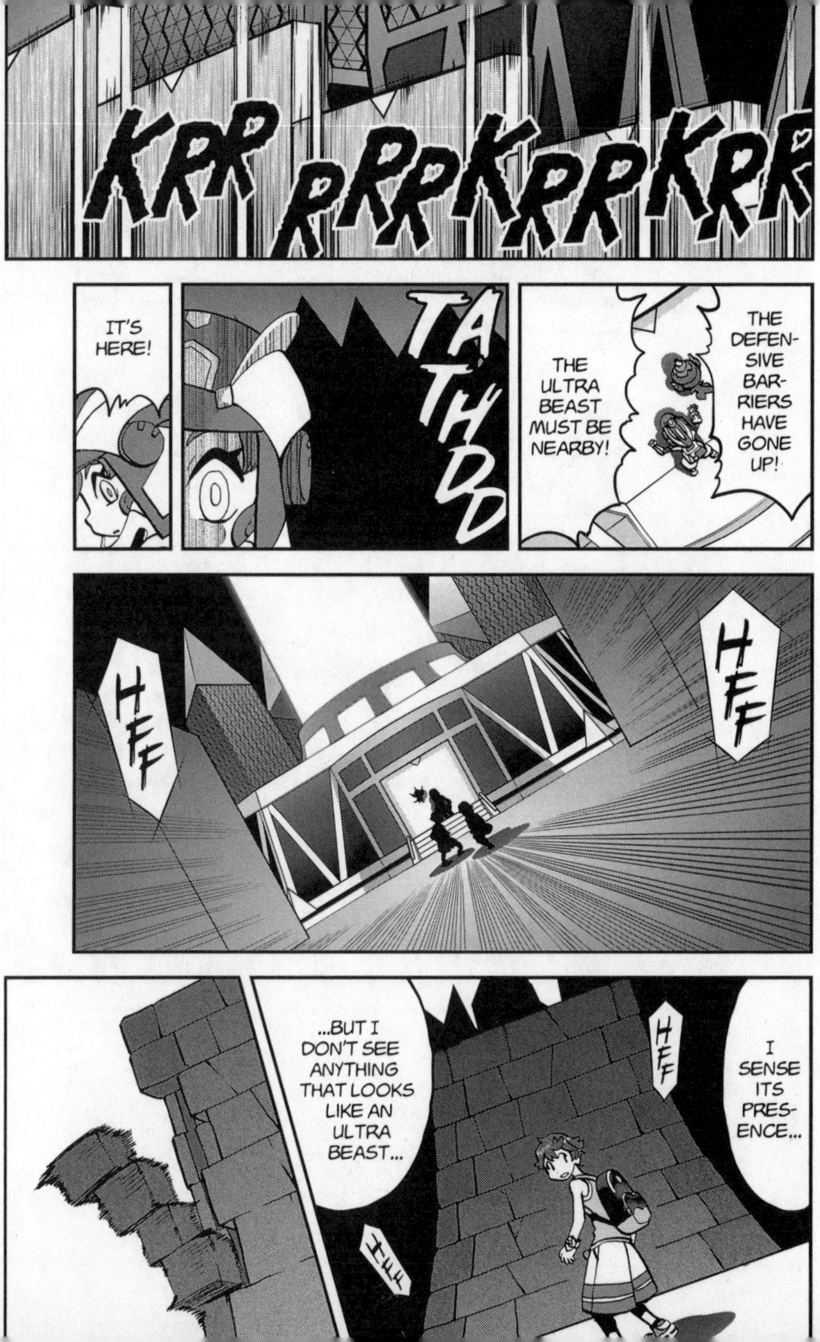
KRP RRPKRPKRR
THE DEFEN-SIVE BAR-RIERS HAVE GONE UP!
THE ULTRA BEAST MUST BE NEARBY!
TATHDD
IT'S HERE!
HFF
HFF
I SENSE ITS PRES-ENCE...
HFF
...BUT I DON'T SEE ANYTHING THAT LOOKS LIKE AN ULTRA BEAST...
HFF

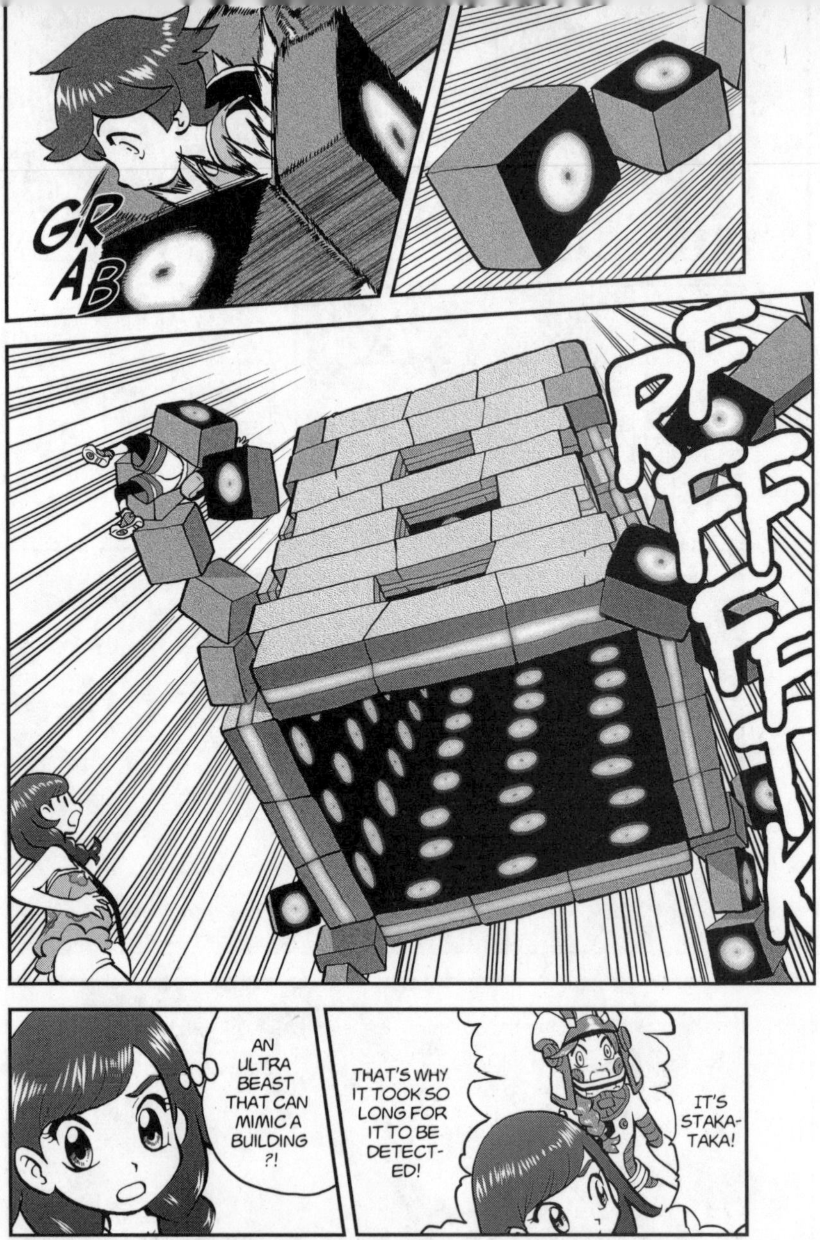
GRAB
RFFFFTK
IT'S STAKA-TAKA!
THAT'S WHY IT TOOK SO LONG FOR IT TO BE DETECT-ED!
AN ULTRA BEAST THAT CAN MIMIC A BUILDING ?!

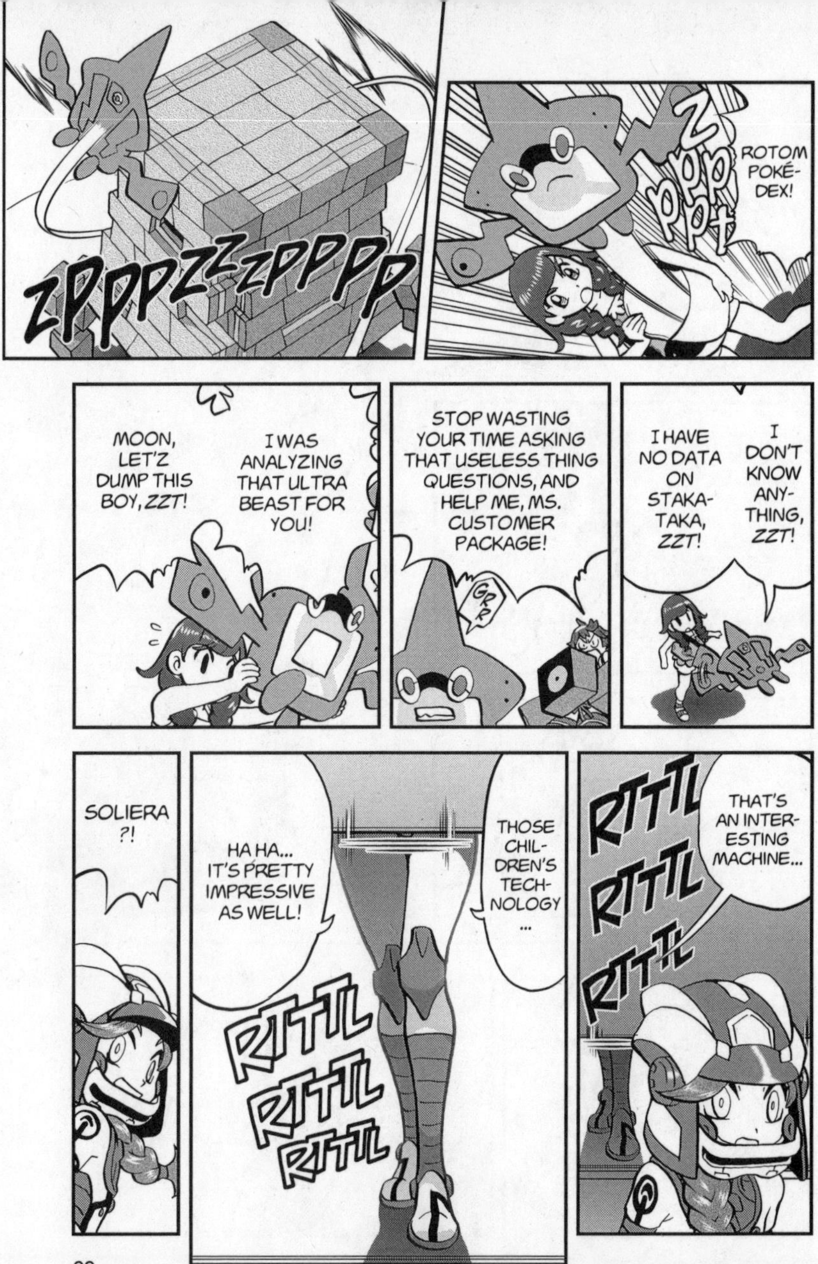
ROTOM POKÉ-DEX!
ZZPPPPPT
ZPPPZZZZPPPPP
I DON'T KNOW ANYTHING, ZZT!
I HAVE NO DATA ON STAKATAKA, ZZT!
STOP WASTING YOUR TIME ASKING THAT USELESS THING QUESTIONS, AND HELP ME, MS. CUSTOMER PACKAGE!
GRR
I WAS ANALYZING THAT ULTRA BEAST FOR YOU!
MOON, LET'Z DUMP THIS BOY, ZZT!
THAT'S AN INTERESTING MACHINE...
RTTTL
RTTTL
RTTTL
THOSE CHILDREN'S TECHNOLOGY...
HA HA... IT'S PRETTY IMPRESSIVE AS WELL!
RTTTL
RTTTL
RTTTL
SOLIERA?!

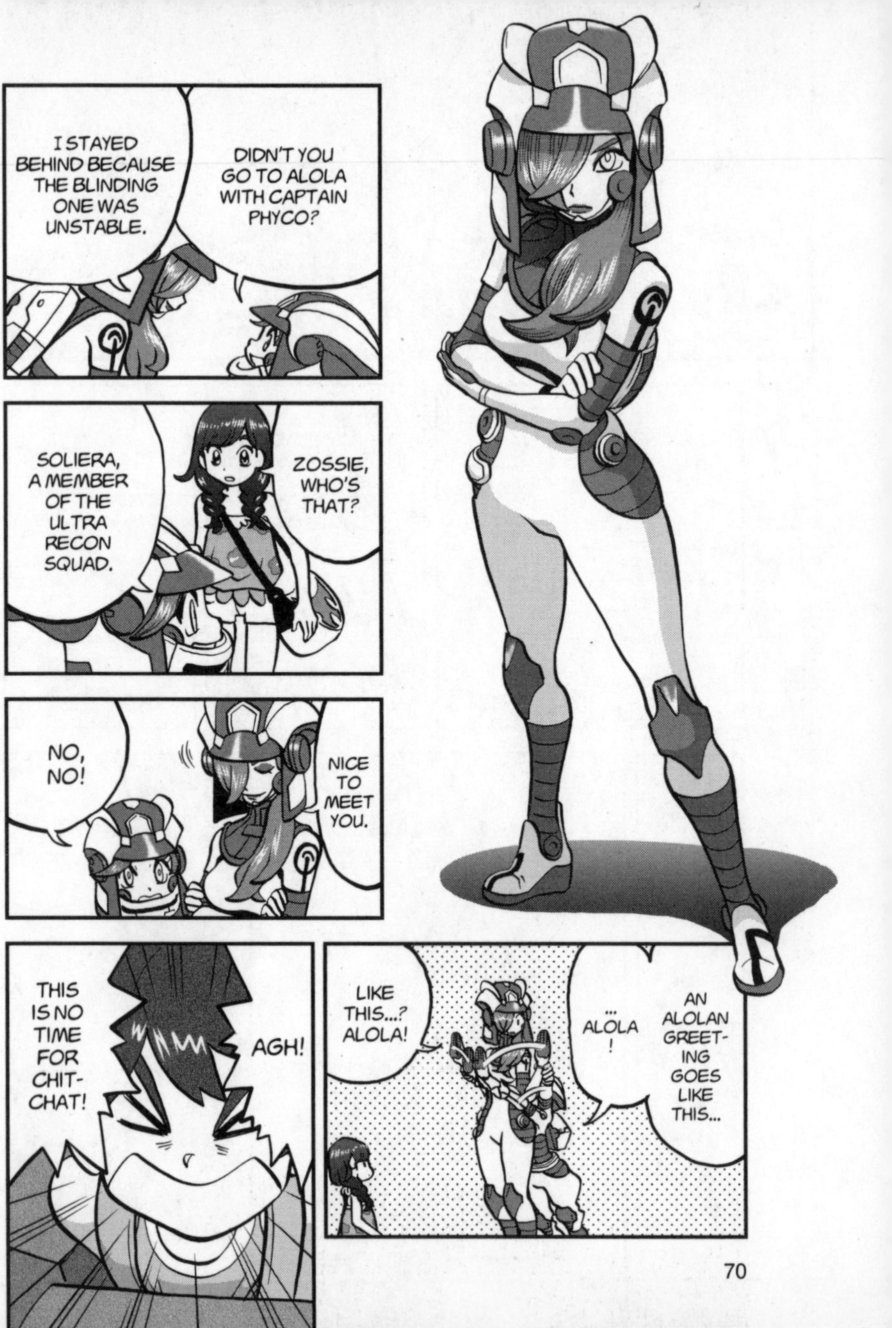
DIDN'T YOU GO TO ALOLA WITH CAPTAIN PHYCO?
I STAYED BEHIND BECAUSE THE BLINDING ONE WAS UNSTABLE.
ZOSSIE, WHO'S THAT?
SOLIERA, A MEMBER OF THE ULTRA RECON SQUAD.
NICE TO MEET YOU.
NO, NO!
AN ALOLAN GREET-ING GOES LIKE THIS...
... ALOLA!
LIKE THIS...? ALOLA!
AGH!
THIS IS NO TIME FOR CHIT-CHAT!

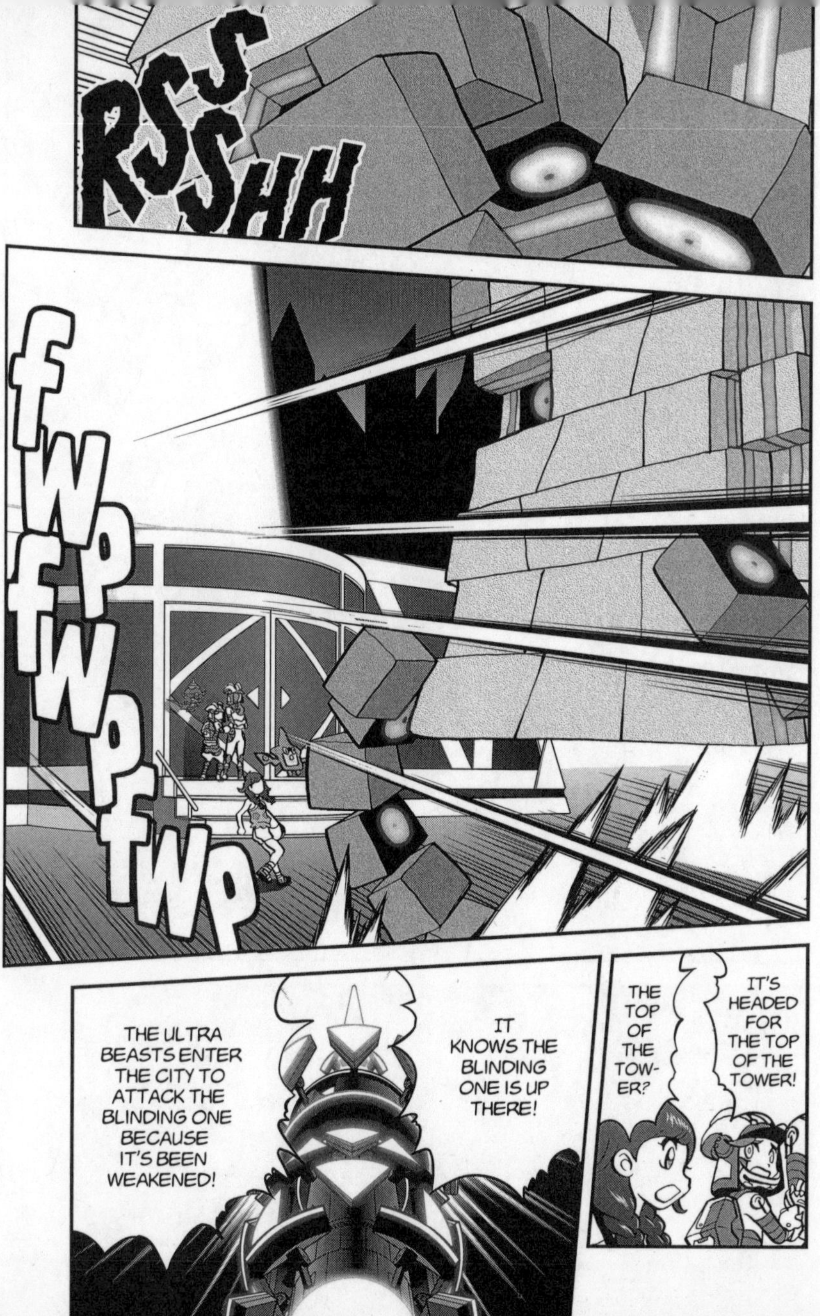
RSSHH
fwp fwp fwp fwp
IT'S HEADED FOR THE TOP OF THE TOWER!
THE TOP OF THE TOW-ER?
IT KNOWS THE BLINDING ONE IS UP THERE!
THE ULTRA BEASTS ENTER THE CITY TO ATTACK THE BLINDING ONE BECAUSE IT'S BEEN WEAKENED!

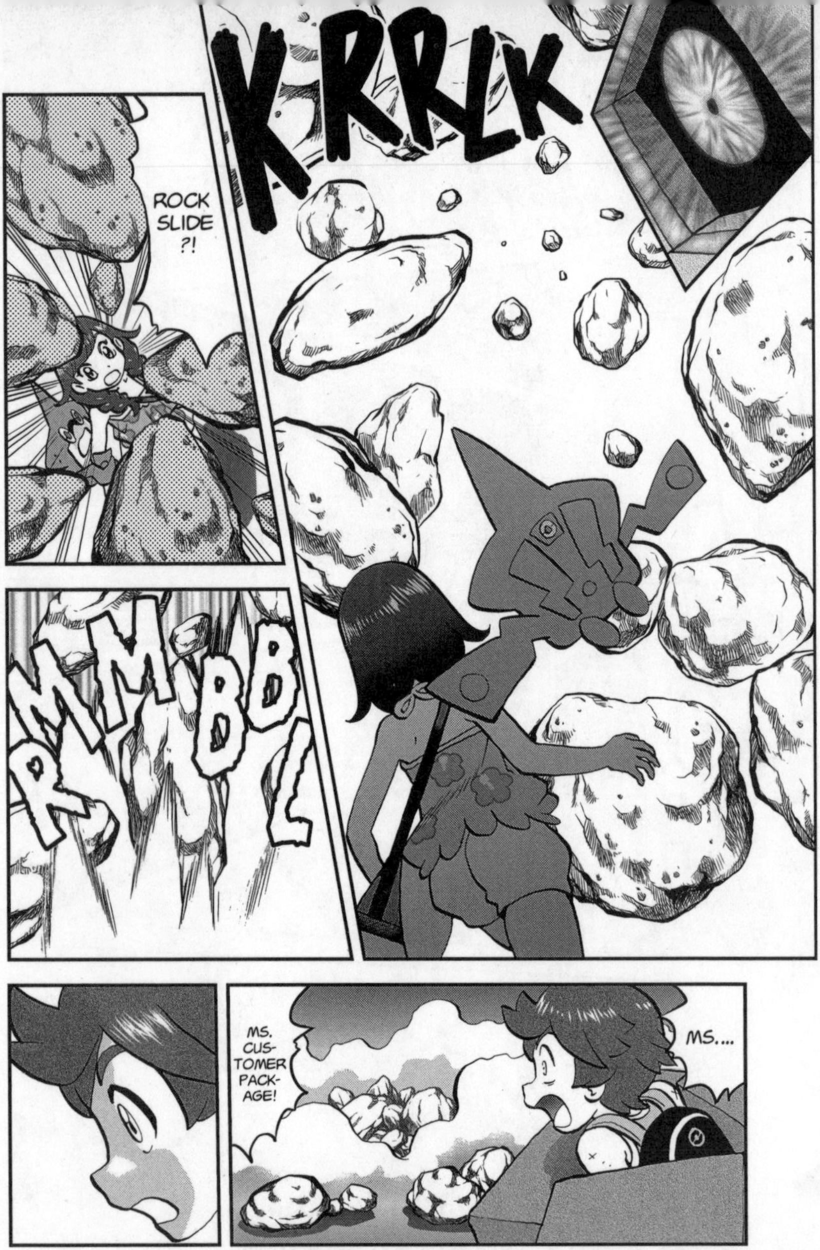
KRRLK
ROCK SLIDE ?!
RMMBBL
MS....
MS. CUS-TOMER PACK-AGE!

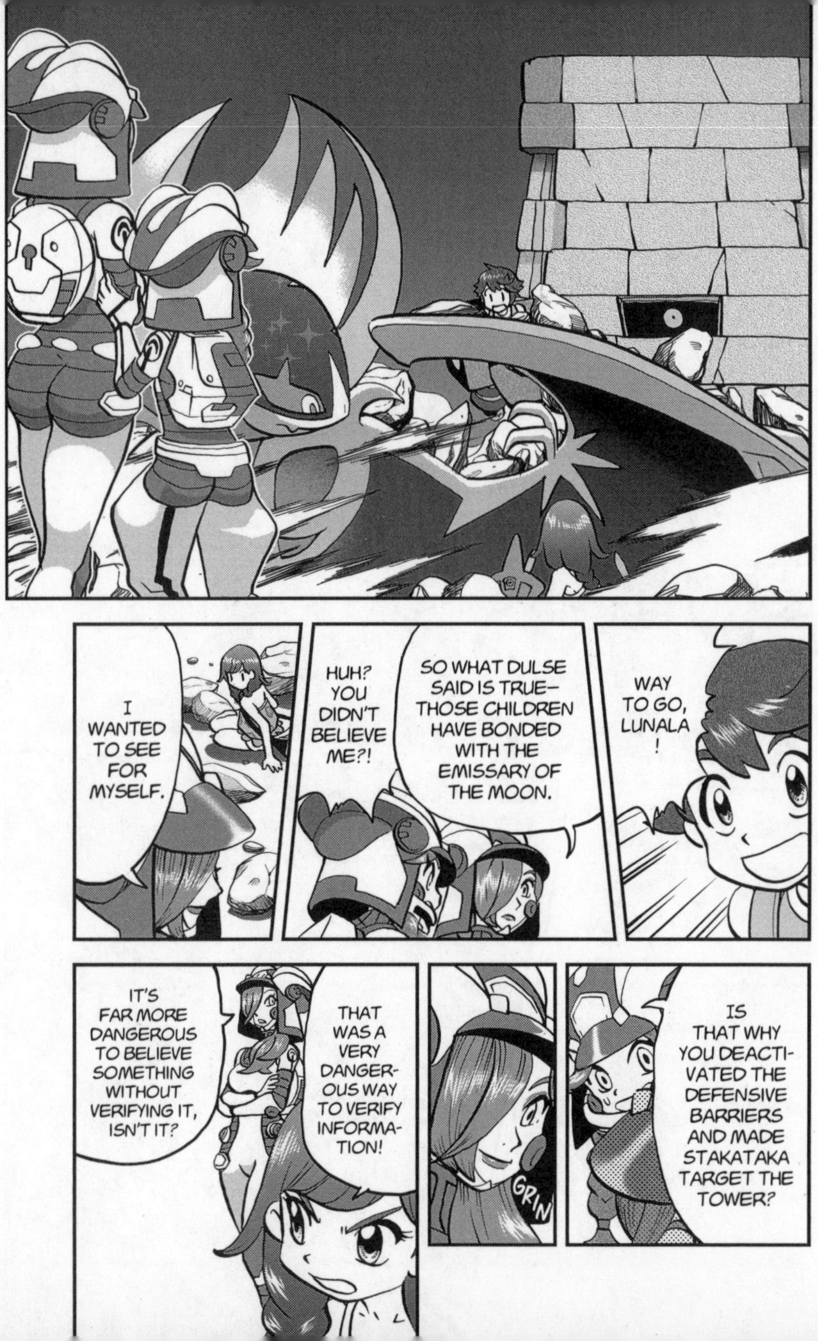
WAY TO GO, LUNALA!
SO WHAT DULSE SAID IS TRUE—THOSE CHILDREN HAVE BONDED WITH THE EMISSARY OF THE MOON.
HUH? YOU DIDN'T BELIEVE ME?!
I WANTED TO SEE FOR MYSELF.
IS THAT WHY YOU DEACTIVATED THE DEFENSIVE BARRIERS AND MADE STAKATAKA TARGET THE TOWER?
GRIN
THAT WAS A VERY DANGEROUS WAY TO VERIFY INFORMATION!
IT'S FAR MORE DANGEROUS TO BELIEVE SOMETHING WITHOUT VERIFYING IT, ISN'T IT?

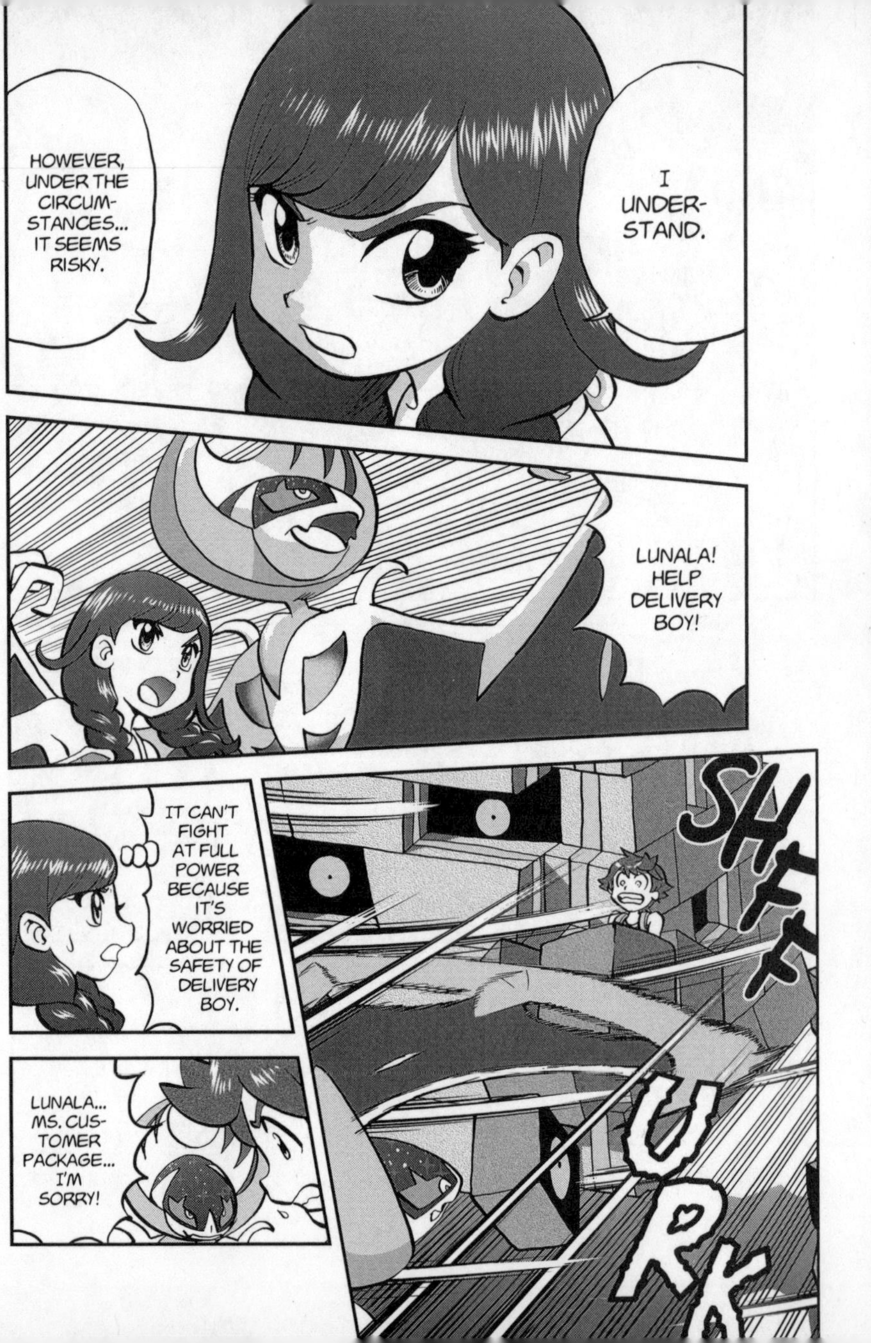
I UNDERSTAND.
HOWEVER, UNDER THE CIRCUMSTANCES... IT SEEMS RISKY.
LUNALA! HELP DELIVERY BOY!
SHFF
URK
IT CAN'T FIGHT AT FULL POWER BECAUSE IT'S WORRIED ABOUT THE SAFETY OF DELIVERY BOY.
LUNALA... MS. CUSTOMER PACKAGE... I'M SORRY!

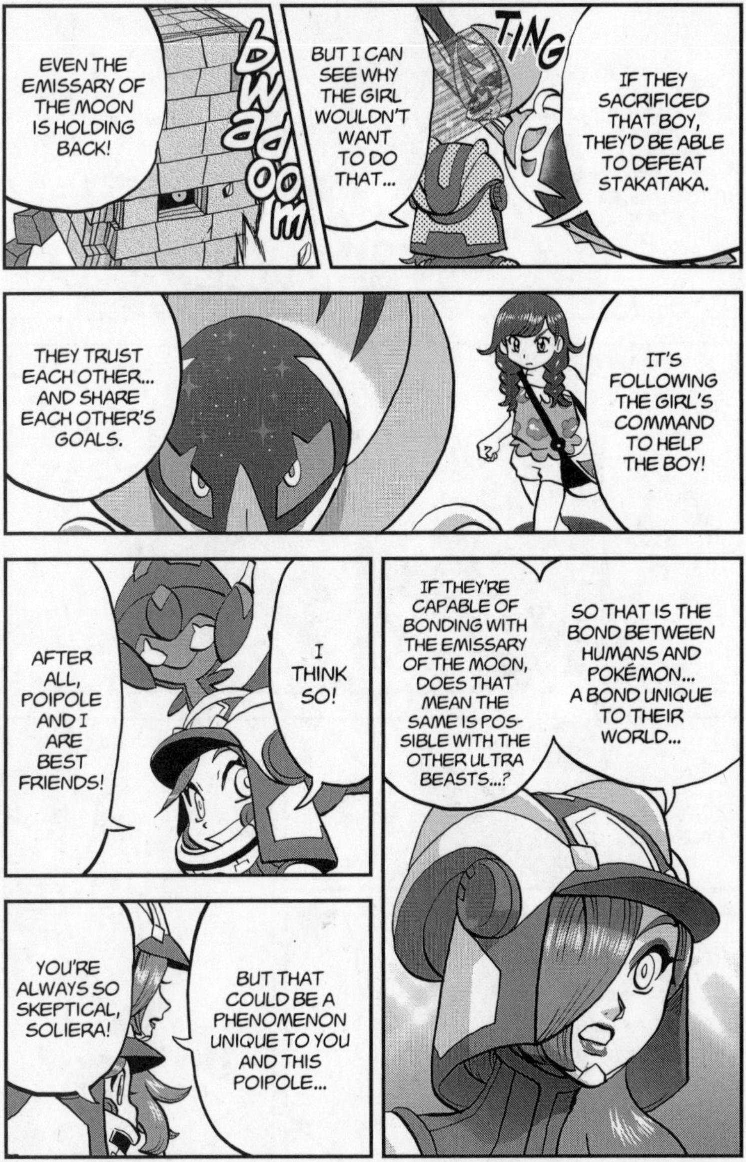
TING
IF THEY SACRIFICED THAT BOY, THEY'D BE ABLE TO DEFEAT STAKATAKA.
BUT I CAN SEE WHY THE GIRL WOULDN'T WANT TO DO THAT...
bwadoom
EVEN THE EMISSARY OF THE MOON IS HOLDING BACK!
IT'S FOLLOWING THE GIRL'S COMMAND TO HELP THE BOY!
THEY TRUST EACH OTHER... AND SHARE EACH OTHER'S GOALS.
SO THAT IS THE BOND BETWEEN HUMANS AND POKÉMON... A BOND UNIQUE TO THEIR WORLD...
IF THEY'RE CAPABLE OF BONDING WITH THE EMISSARY OF THE MOON, DOES THAT MEAN THE SAME IS POS-SIBLE WITH THE OTHER ULTRA BEASTS...?
I THINK SO!
AFTER ALL, POIPOLE AND I ARE BEST FRIENDS!
BUT THAT COULD BE A PHENOMENON UNIQUE TO YOU AND THIS POIPOLE...
YOU'RE ALWAYS SO SKEPTICAL, SOLIERA!

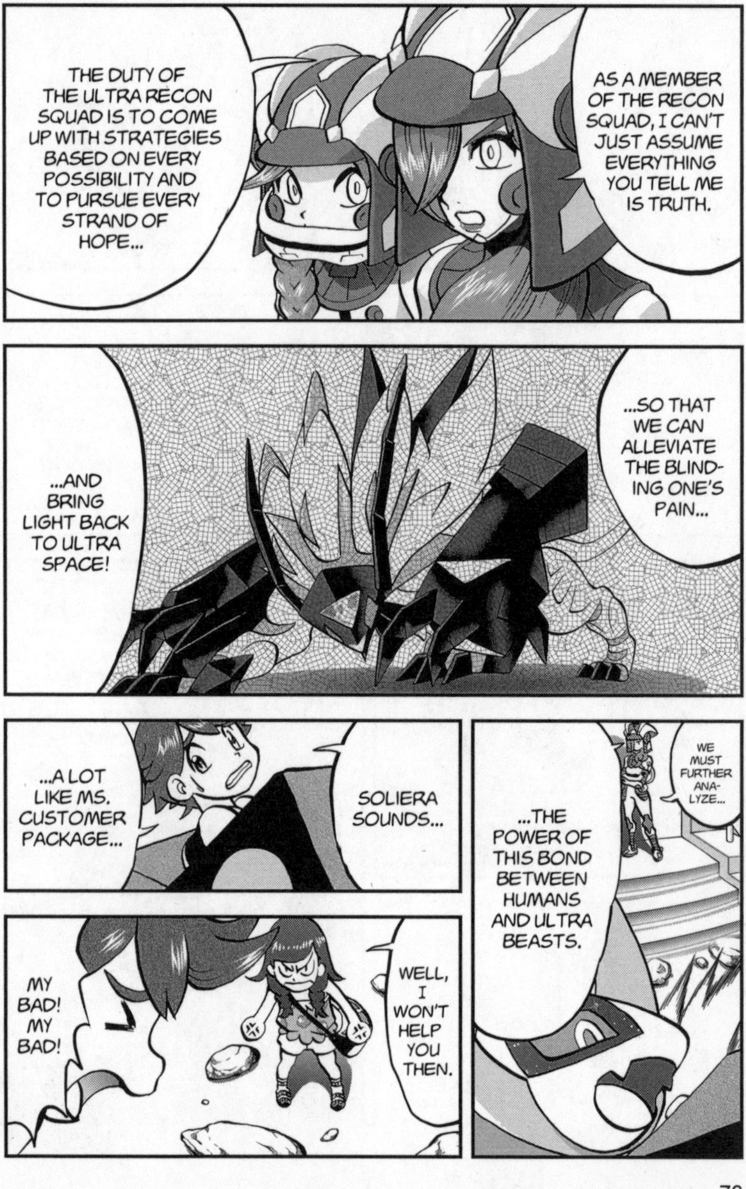
AS A MEMBER OF THE RECON SQUAD, I CAN'T JUST ASSUME EVERYTHING YOU TELL ME IS TRUTH.
THE DUTY OF THE ULTRA RECON SQUAD IS TO COME UP WITH STRATEGIES BASED ON EVERY POSSIBILITY AND TO PURSUE EVERY STRAND OF HOPE...
...SO THAT WE CAN ALLEVIATE THE BLIND-ING ONE'S PAIN...
...AND BRING LIGHT BACK TO ULTRA SPACE!
WE MUST FURTHER ANA-LYZE...
...THE POWER OF THIS BOND BETWEEN HUMANS AND ULTRA BEASTS.
SOLIERA SOUNDS...
...A LOT LIKE MS. CUSTOMER PACKAGE...
WELL, I WON'T HELP YOU THEN.
MY BAD! MY BAD!

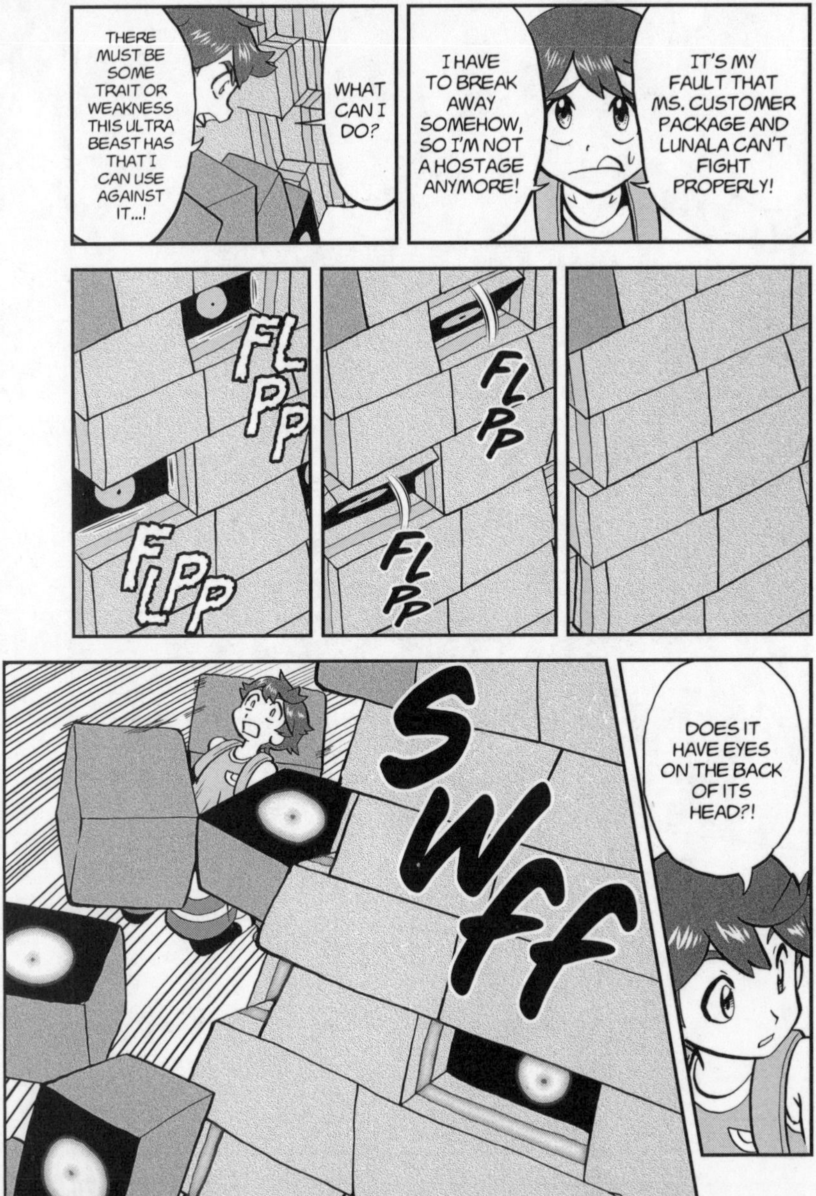
IT'S MY FAULT THAT MS. CUSTOMER PACKAGE AND LUNALA CAN'T FIGHT PROPERLY!
I HAVE TO BREAK AWAY SOMEHOW, SO I'M NOT A HOSTAGE ANYMORE!
WHAT CAN I DO?
THERE MUST BE SOME TRAIT OR WEAKNESS THIS ULTRA BEAST HAS THAT I CAN USE AGAINST IT...!
FLPP
FLPP
FLPP
FLPP
DOES IT HAVE EYES ON THE BACK OF ITS HEAD?!
SWFF

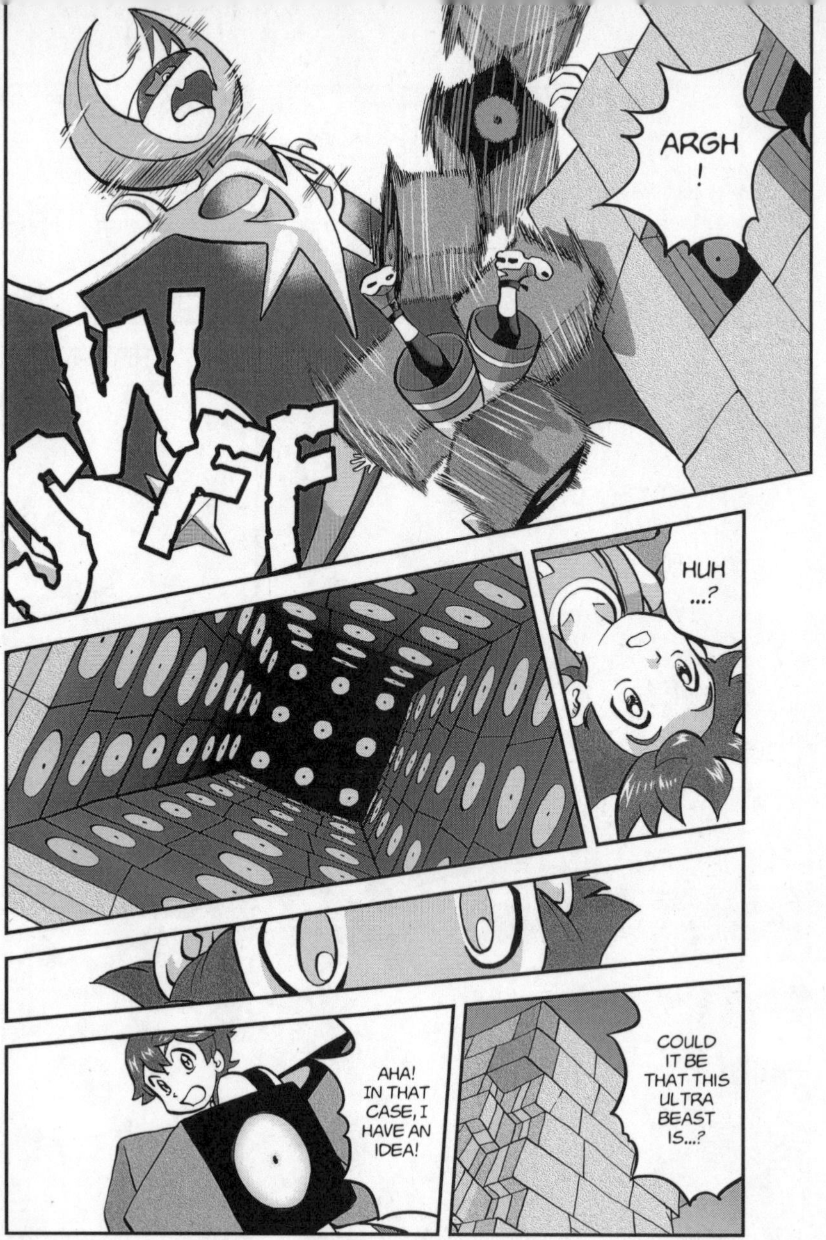
ARGH
!
SWFF
HUH
...?
COULD IT BE THAT THIS ULTRA BEAST IS...?
AHA! IN THAT CASE, I HAVE AN IDEA!

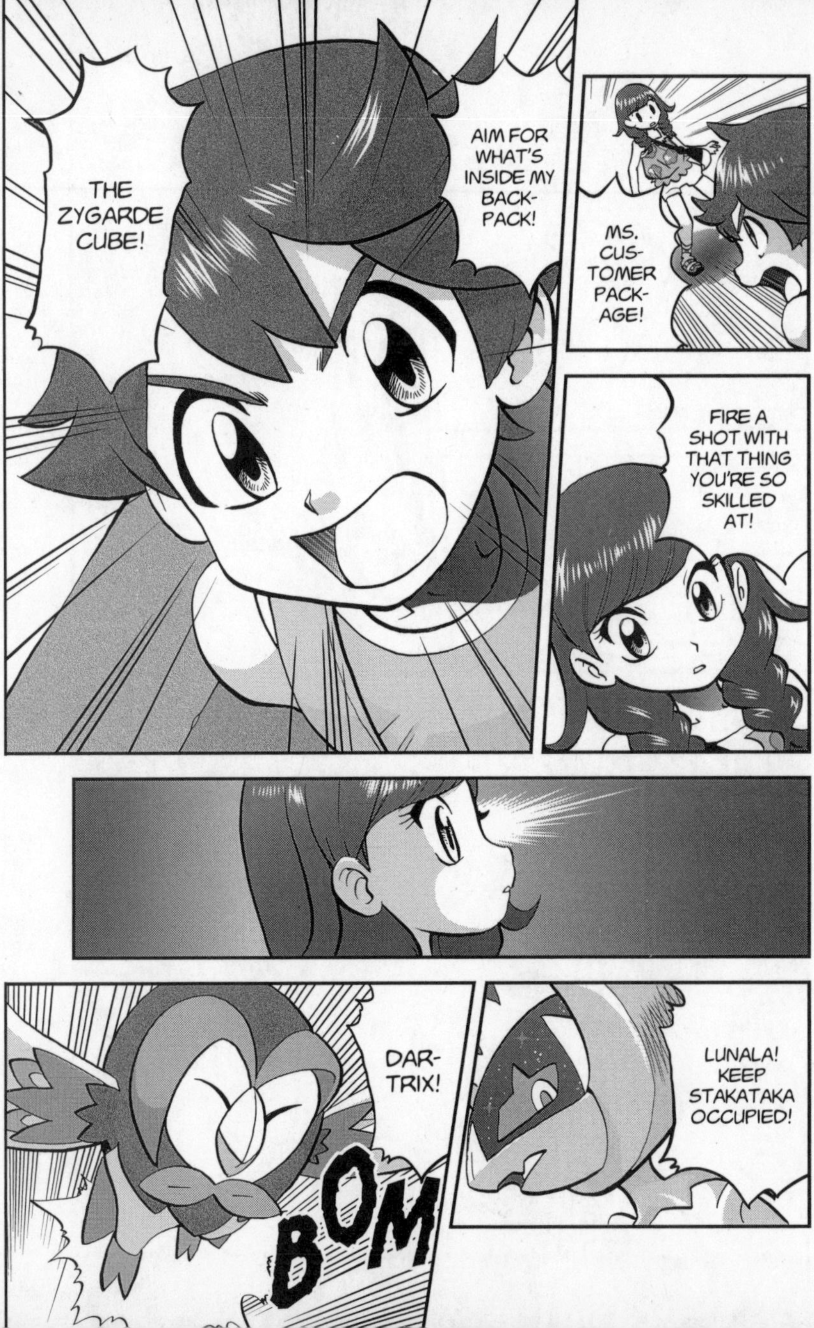
MS. CUS-TOMER PACK-AGE!
FIRE A SHOT WITH THAT THING YOU'RE SO SKILLED AT!
AIM FOR WHAT'S INSIDE MY BACK-PACK!
THE ZYGARDE CUBE!
LUNALA! KEEP STAKATAKA OCCUPIED!
DAR-TRIX!
BOM

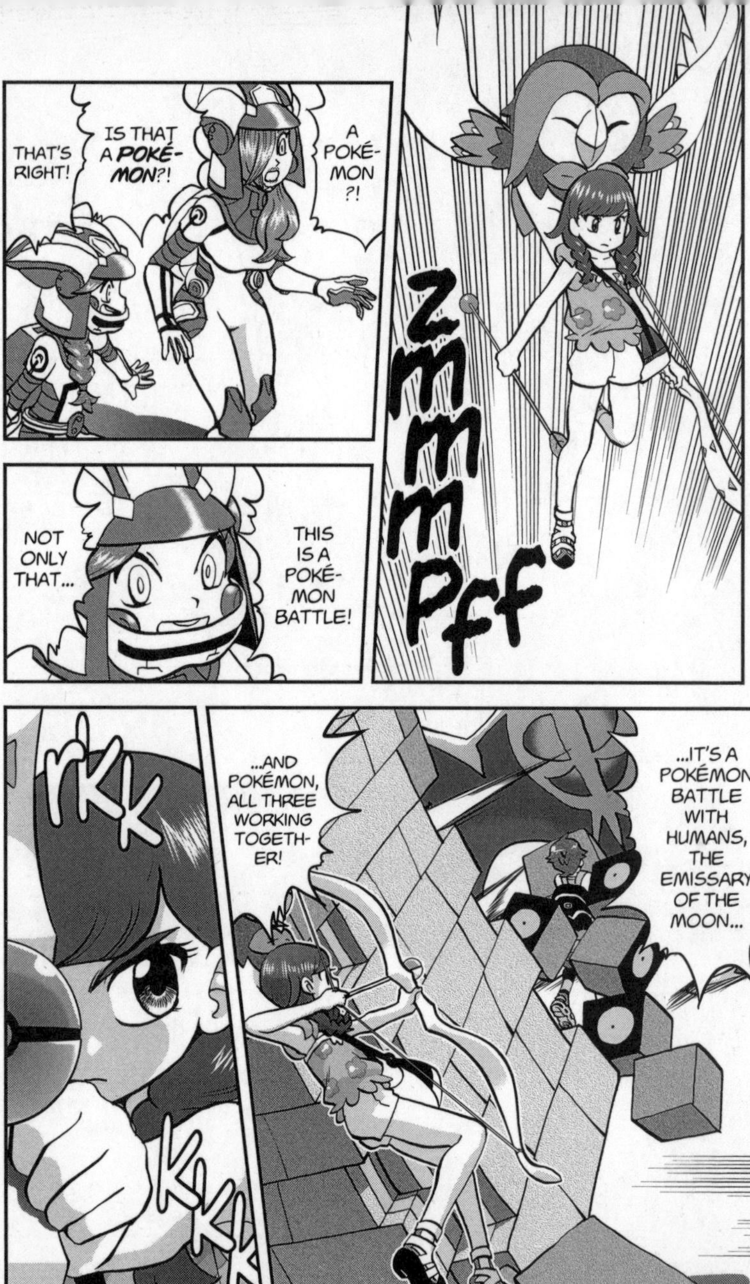
ZMMMPFF
A POKÉ-MON?!
IS THAT A POKÉMON?!
THAT'S RIGHT!
THIS IS A POKÉMON BATTLE!
NOT ONLY THAT...
...IT'S A POKÉMON BATTLE WITH HUMANS, THE EMISSARY OF THE MOON...
...AND POKÉMON, ALL THREE WORKING TOGETHER!
rKK
KKKK

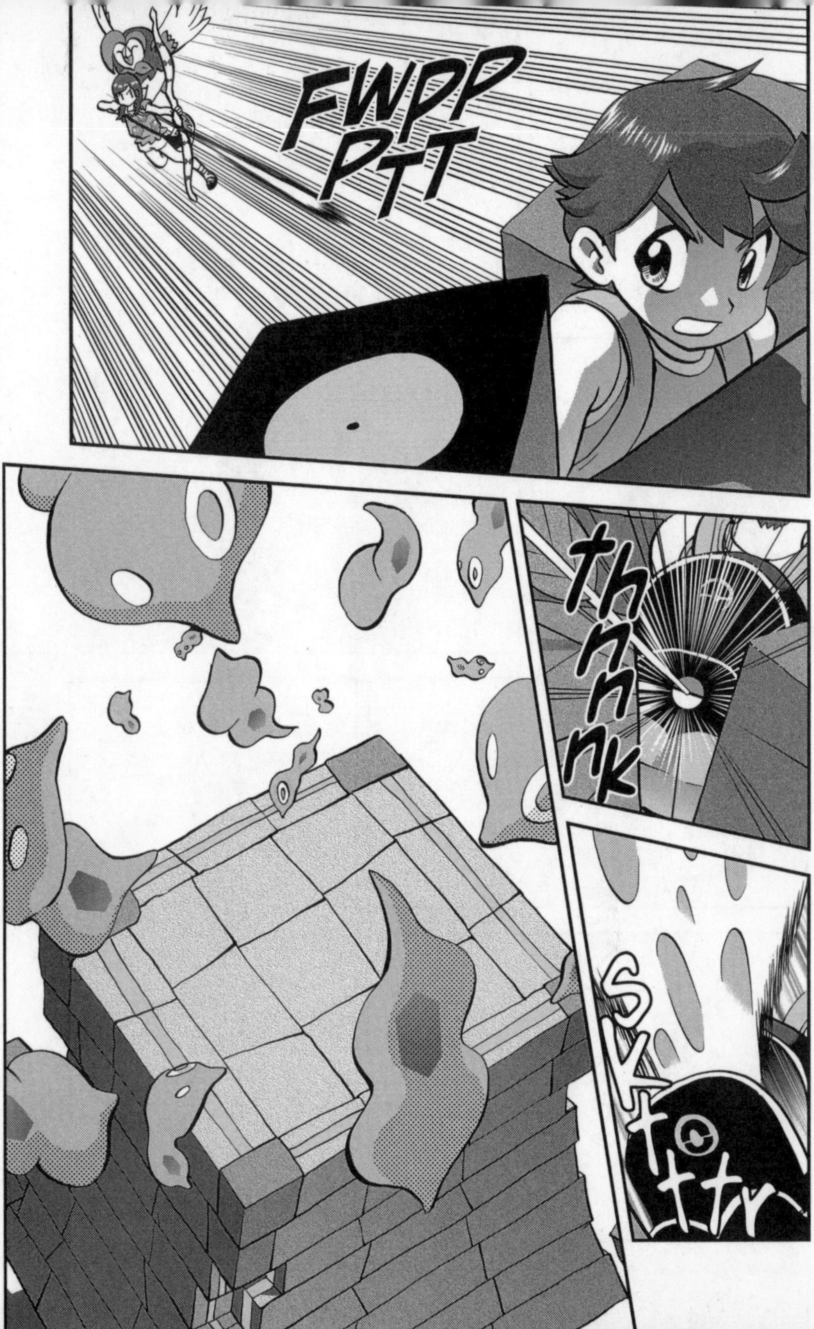
FWPP PTT
thnnnk
sktttr

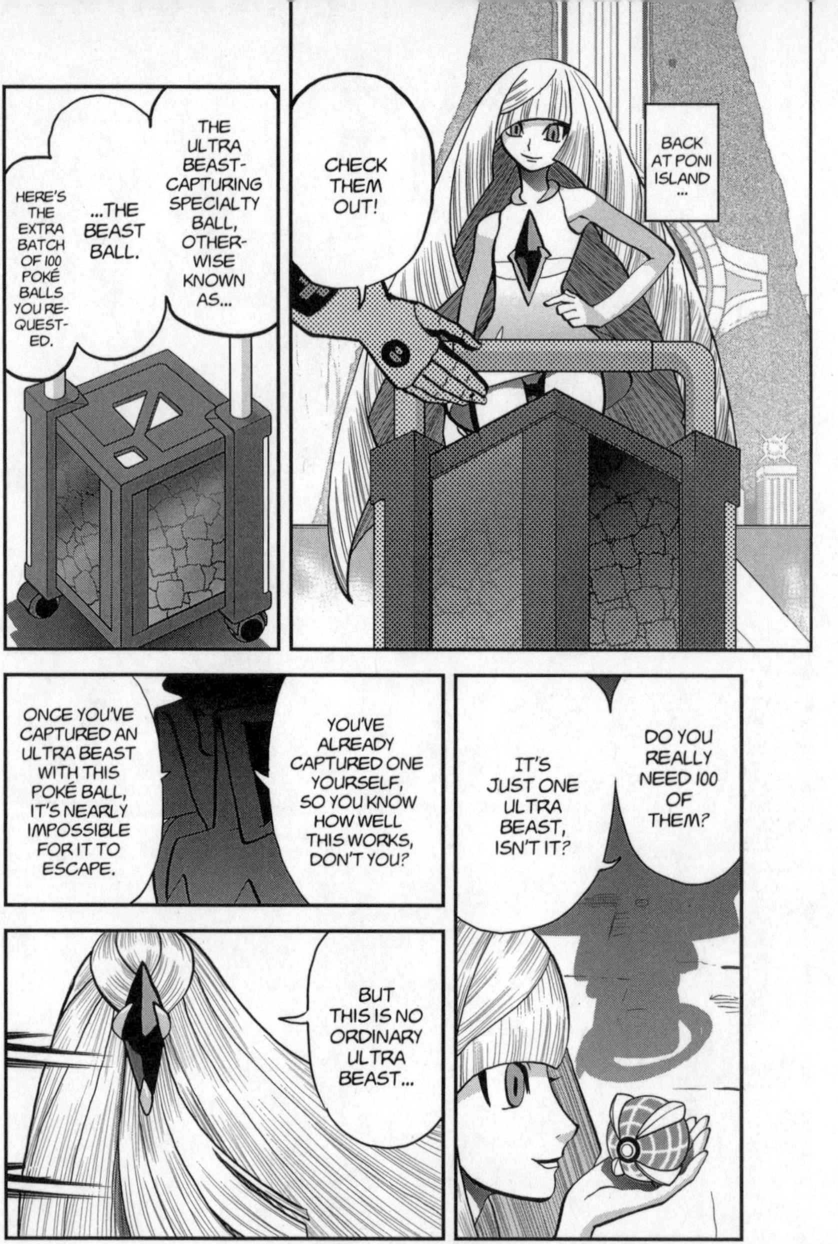
BACK AT PONI ISLAND ...
CHECK THEM OUT!
THE ULTRA BEAST-CAPTURING SPECIALTY BALL, OTHERWISE KNOWN AS...
...THE BEAST BALL.
HERE'S THE EXTRA BATCH OF 100 POKÉ BALLS YOU REQUESTED.
DO YOU REALLY NEED 100 OF THEM?
IT'S JUST ONE ULTRA BEAST, ISN'T IT?
YOU'VE ALREADY CAPTURED ONE YOURSELF, SO YOU KNOW HOW WELL THIS WORKS, DON'T YOU?
ONCE YOU'VE CAPTURED AN ULTRA BEAST WITH THIS POKÉ BALL, IT'S NEARLY IMPOSSIBLE FOR IT TO ESCAPE.
BUT THIS IS NO ORDINARY ULTRA BEAST...

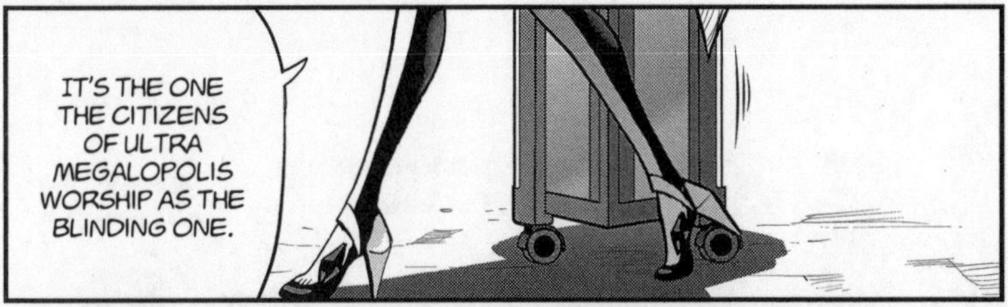
IT'S THE ONE THE CITIZENS OF ULTRA MEGALOPOLIS WORSHIP AS THE BLINDING ONE.

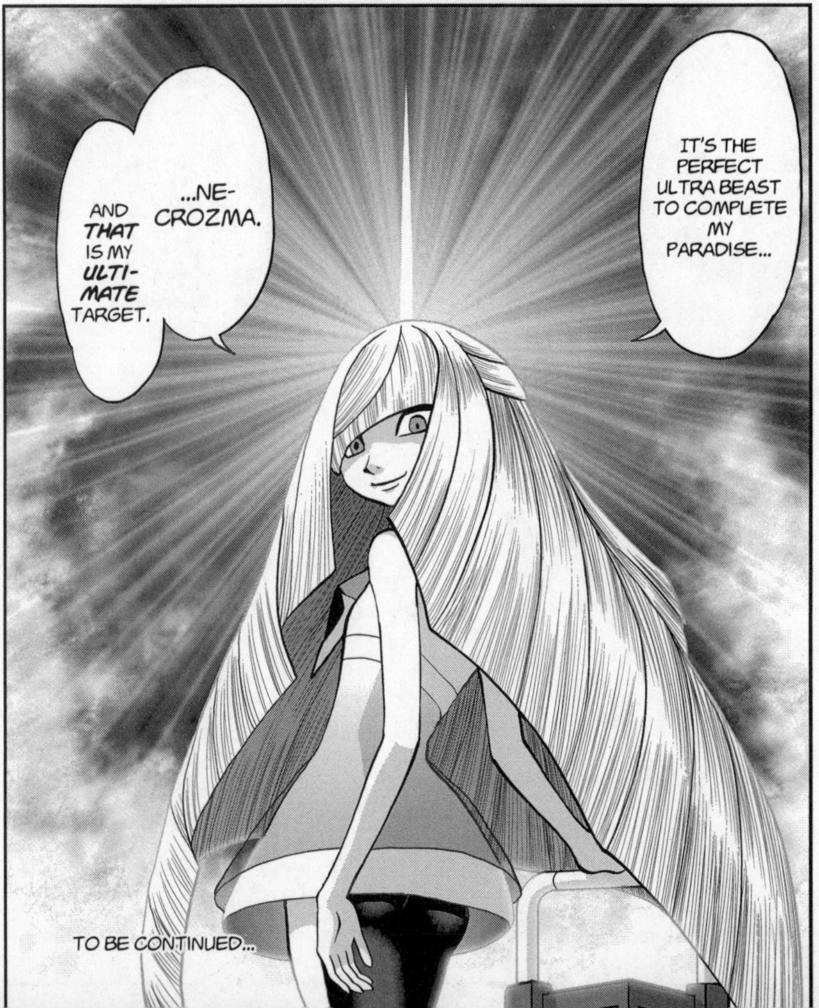
IT'S THE PERFECT ULTRA BEAST TO COMPLETE MY PARADISE...
...NE-CROZMA.
AND *THAT* IS MY *ULTIMATE* TARGET.
TO BE CONTINUED...

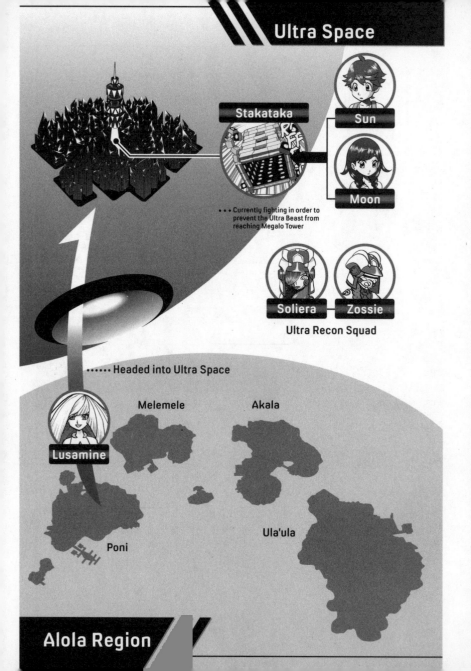

Stakataka

Sun

Moon

··· Currently fighting in order to
prevent the Ultra Beast from
reaching Megalo Tower

Soliera — Zossie

Ultra Recon Squad

······ Headed into Ultra Space

Melemele

Akala

Lusamine

Poni

Ula'ula

Alola Region

**Pokémon Sun & Moon
Volume 9
VIZ Media Edition**

Story by HIDENORI KUSAKA
Art by SATOSHI YAMAMOTO

©2021 Pokémon.
©1995–2019 Nintendo / Creatures Inc. / GAME FREAK inc.
TM, ®, and character names are trademarks of Nintendo.
POCKET MONSTERS SPECIAL SUN • MOON Vol. 5
by Hidenori KUSAKA, Satoshi YAMAMOTO
© 2017 Hidenori KUSAKA, Satoshi YAMAMOTO
All rights reserved.
Original Japanese edition published by SHOGAKUKAN.
English translation rights in the United States of America, Canada, the United Kingdom,
Ireland, Australia and New Zealand arranged with SHOGAKUKAN.

Original Cover Design—Hiroyuki KAWASOME (grafio)

English Adaptation—Bryant Turnage
Translation—Tetsuichiro Miyaki
Touch-Up & Lettering—Susan Daigle-Leach
Design—Alice Lewis
Editors—Annette Roman, Joel Enos

Printed in the U.S.A.

Published by
VIZ Media, LLC
P.O. Box 77010
San Francisco, CA 94107

10 9 8 7 6 5 4 3 2 1
First printing, January 2021

viz.com

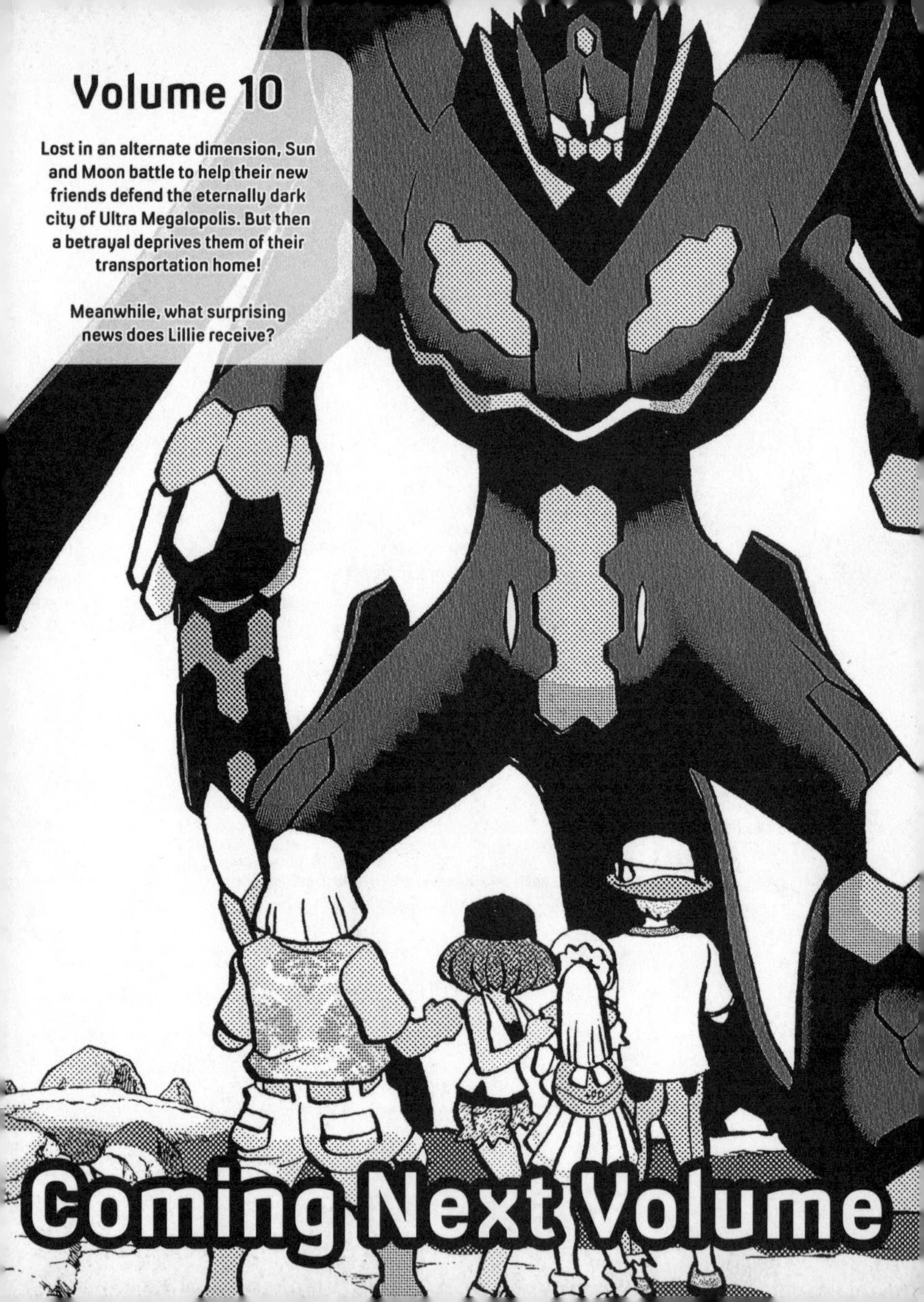
Volume 10
Lost in an alternate dimension, Sun and Moon battle to help their new friends defend the eternally dark city of Ultra Megalopolis. But then a betrayal deprives them of their transportation home!
Meanwhile, what surprising news does Lillie receive?
Coming Next Volume

THIS IS THE END OF THIS GRAPHIC NOVEL!

To properly enjoy this VIZ Media graphic novel, please turn it around and begin reading from right to left.

This book has been printed in the original Japanese format in order to preserve the orientation of the original artwork. Have fun with it!

<<<
READ THIS WAY!

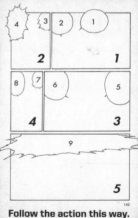

Follow the action this way.